Wormwood Echoes

LAKEN CANE

Copyright © 2015 Laken Cane

All rights reserved.

The author acknowledges the trademark status and trademark owners of various products referenced in this work of fiction, which have been used without permission. The publication/use of these trademarks is not authorized, association with, or sponsored by the trademark owners.

This book or any portion thereof may not be reproduced or used in any manner whatsoever without the express written permission of the publisher except for the use of brief quotations in a book review.

ISBN-10: 151414719X

ISBN-13 978-1514147191:

DEDICATION

I wanted to keep listing the names of everyone I'd like to dedicate these books to, but the list is so very long and I'm terrified I'll leave someone out!
So this book is for all the fans—you make me so happy to be a writer. For my fan club, crew, and street team—my Crewsaders. You are such bright spots in my days. For all the people who pimp my books, work incredibly hard to promote me, and are so very dedicated.
A writer's life can be lonely. You all make that far from the truth for me.
I thank you for the cards, the gifts, the feedback, the listening, the shoulders, and the enthusiasm.
Thank you for taking time to write reviews, Facebook friending me, telling others about the books, and messaging me to check on me. Thank you for writing me to say how much you love the characters and the world in which they live.
This book is for you.
Thank you, Team Berserker, and thank you, Team Owen. Your discussions are lively, entertaining, and really do make me LOL. A lot.
Thank you for being my friends. I treasure you.
This book is for you.
And thank you, my Z Girl.
This book is for you.

Part One

THE DAWNING

CHAPTER ONE

She ran through Wormwood, her heart heavier with each step she took.

Gunnar the Ghoul was gone.

He'd fled his home for fear of the assassin.

That was her fault.

She should have killed the assassin. She should have taken his head to Gunnar.

She hadn't, though, and after she'd lost her own head and lay mending for a fucking *month*, Gunnar had fled.

He'd figured she'd abandoned him, maybe, and she had no way of telling him otherwise. Her crew had been too concerned for her and busy protecting the city to think of the ghoul.

She stopped running, threw back her head, and

screamed, "Gunnar!"

Her voice echoed through the vast graveyard like the wail of agony it was, and when she got no answer she fell to her knees.

She had lost him, and it hurt like a motherfucker.

Alone but for the moon, she allowed herself to cry, to mourn.

"Gunnar," she whispered.

She'd searched Wormwood for three weeks, every single night, hoping he'd appear in front of her, hands reaching for his Baby Ruth candy bars.

Your Highness...

She pulled a bag from her pocket and placed it carefully on the ground.

Gunnar wasn't coming.

He'd always been there.

But he wasn't coming.

She wanted to get angry at his...his *abandonment*, but how could she? She hadn't killed the fucking assassin.

She jerked her head up at a sudden, barely there sound that let her know she had company.

Simon Kelic rushed with stealthy speed into the clearing, making her believe for one heart stopping second that Gunnar had returned.

Crushing disappointment followed the surge of hope.

And that pissed her off.

He had his children at his back—at least some of them—and his exotic favorite, Iker, at his side.

She climbed to her feet, leaving the bag of Baby Ruth candy bars on the ground.

Just in case.

Iker, as curious—or nosy—as a child, leaned over and reached for the bag.

"Fuck off," she told him.

"Girl, you are starting to—"

"Iker," Simon said, his voice tired.

"I know, I know." Iker held up his hands and backed

away, glaring at Rune the entire time. "Mustn't upset the princess."

"The only princess here is you, dude." Then she ignored him and looked at the vampire master. "What do you want, Kelic?"

She held her breath, hoping with every part of her that he'd say he knew where Gunnar was.

He didn't.

"There's something wrong with one of my vampires. I have come to ask you to look at her."

"I'm not a doctor."

"Please, Rune." He hesitated. "I'm worried."

"What do you think I can do? Ask me to feed her and I'm kicking your ass."

"I'd never suggest that. And I don't know. We don't get sick. But…there's something wrong. Something terrible."

"Besides," Iker said, unable to remain quiet, "this shit could spread. You're responsible for the Others, so get your ass to responsibilizing."

She softened, just the slightest bit, because fuck if Iker's stupid word didn't make her think of Gunnar. "Fine," she said. "Take me to her."

Simon tossed a quick look of admiration at Iker, whose black eyes held a spark of smug pride. Yeah, they were playing her, but fuck them. The young vampire wasn't wrong. She *was* responsible for the Others.

She followed Simon to the outskirts of Spiritgrove, to a quietly bland, unremarkable house. It was large, true, but looked nothing like the gothic nightmares Nicolas Llodra had preferred.

It was a white two-story on Mills street, with a weeping willow tree in the middle of the well-kept yard. There was even a white picket fence.

"You're trying a little too hard," she murmured. She swept the area with her narrowed gaze, picking apart dark shadows the moon and streetlights did little to illuminate.

He shrugged. "I'm a simple man, Rune. I like home and family as much as the next guy."

She laughed.

The interior of the house was nearly as ordinary as the outside. Other than the fact that it was a lot more crowded, it wasn't that different from *her* home.

People—vampires, mostly—sat on couches and the floor watching a giant flat screen TV. There was an animated movie playing, and the watchers seemed completely immersed. They looked up at the newcomers' entrance, then went right back to their movie.

"Dude," Rune said. "That's fucked up."

"Why?" Simon sounded the tiniest bit amused.

"She thinks we should all be out drinking blood and having orgies," Iker said. "She's lost touch with her own kind."

And for once, he didn't sound angry. He sounded almost…sad.

She might have to rethink her impression of the remarkable Iker.

"But we're not really her own kind," Simon said, gently. "Any more than the humans are."

She said nothing.

She had no kind.

Then they walked from the living room into a huge kitchen, and Rune breathed a sigh of relief.

Three vampires had their human bite junkies spread across the enormous wooden table and were busy having dinner. The junkies, two females and one male, were naked and dirty.

As she watched, one of the junkies opened her eyes a little and saw Rune. "Oh," she said, pushing at the vampire on top of her. "It's Rune Alexander."

He growled and pulled his fangs from her groin. His glance at Rune was not friendly. "Yeah?" he said. "So?"

"So I wouldn't mind giving her a little taste, Bobby. Get off me."

"I told you not to call me that. My name is Robert. *Robert.*"

"Don't worry, Robert Robert," Rune said. "I'm not taking her up on her offer." She gave them a sharp nod. "As you were."

"Your mood has lifted since we entered the front door," Simon said. "May I ask why?"

"Because that," Rune said, pointing at the table of vampires and junkies, "is something I understand. A room full of bloodsuckers watching Shrek is not."

"Haven't you noticed the changes to this county since we arrived?" Iker was back to his usual cantankerous self. "My master has cleaned up your city. You have no idea because you're all wrapped up in your precious princess self."

Rune faced the young vampire, waving off Simon when he started to rebuke his charge. She stared at the boy for a long moment, acknowledging the sudden heavy silence in the room.

Iker's gaze was steady, but deep in his eyes she saw a sudden spark of fear.

She smiled.

"I'm a patient princess, kid, but if you push me too far I will hurt you. I will make you afraid. Terrified." She stepped closer. Got into his space. "You'll want to chill the fuck out." She showed him her monster, just for the briefest second.

Iker opened his mouth, but nothing came out. Not so much as a whisper.

Simon nodded approvingly. "I did warn you. Go to the basement and stay there until I summon you."

Iker didn't argue. He turned and left the kitchen and never once looked back.

Simon inclined his head. "He's a handful."

"And your favorite. I bet he's got quite a story." She hesitated. "Don't torture him."

Simon paused at a doorway leading from the kitchen.

"Torture him? Why would I torture him?"

"For being a disrespectful little son of a bitch?"

He stared. "I'd heard stories of Nicolas Llodra. He was mad, sadistic. I am not. He and I are no more alike than…than he and *you*. His ways are not mine."

Feeling as though she'd just been taken to task by the master, she shrugged and nodded. "Where's your sick vampire?"

"Just through here." He led her from the kitchen, down a rather dark hallway, and finally, he pushed open the door to a spacious room painted in soothing blues and whites.

It could have been mistaken for a human's room, except for three things.

The boarded over window to reject the sun, the large, ornate coffin in the middle of the floor, and a stench so foul she very nearly refused to continue into the room.

It wasn't just a bad smell. It wasn't even the scent of death.

It was a scent she'd never caught before, and it scared the fuck out of her.

Something was very, very wrong inside that room.

CHAPTER TWO

"My God," she said, her hand to her nose. The stench was unbearable. "What the hell is that?"

"She's rotting." Simon walked into the room and calmly opened the coffin lid, which made the smell a hundred times worse.

He remained there, staring down into the foul depths, though the horrible smell had to have been attacking his brain.

She understood.

Had it been one of hers sick or wounded, she'd have done the same.

"Why?" She hesitated, then went to peer into the coffin.

The woman lying there had been around twenty-five when she'd turned, and though dark patches of rot appeared on her cheeks and forehead, they couldn't hide her beauty.

Her hair was dark and thick, framing a heart shaped face with almond eyes and full lips. She was quiet, but aware.

She watched Simon with a gaze so full of trust it made Rune consider that the new master really wasn't such a bad dude.

Even if he *was* a soulless vampire.

"Master," the girl whispered.

Her lower lip split when she spoke. Blood didn't squeeze through the fissures on her newly torn lip—rot did. Purplish-black rot popped out in a putrid mess and slid down her chin like jelly.

Rune pressed a hand to her stomach, hoping she could keep her dinner down.

Simon caressed the girl's face with the back of his hand, gently. "Shhh, Anna. Rest easy, love."

She immediately closed her eyes and slept.

He lowered the coffin lid and then beckoned to Rune. "Come into my sitting room. I'll have coffee brought in." For a second, a flash of envy streaked across his face.

"You miss it," she said.

"Yes," he agreed. "Like I miss the sun." Then he shrugged. "It is the price of immortality."

"Would you trade your immortality for the sun?" She walked into a small room and sat in the chair he indicated.

He threw the question back at her. "Would you?"

"If I had to give up coffee? Hell yeah."

"But then," he said, his voice smooth and dark, "you don't have to, do you? You have everything."

She crossed her legs. "Do I? I think dying a normal death when I'm eighty is preferable to immortality. I've never wanted it."

"That's because your brain is still human." He sat down on the chair across from her. "That will change with time."

She shuddered. "You brought me here to talk about Anna, so let's talk about Anna."

He inclined his head, ever respectful, ever agreeable. He didn't look like a vampire. He looked like a salesman or maybe a high school English teacher. But the vampire was there—one just had to look a little harder to see it.

"First, your coffee." He smiled at her as one of his human tools brought a tray into the room and sat it carefully on the table between them. "I get pleasure from smelling it, even if I can't drink it."

She accepted the cup the young human offered her and

took a tentative sip. "It's good."

"You sound surprised. We're not savages in this coven, Rune."

"Rune," the human interrupted. "Please. Bite me." She fell to her knees at Rune's side, pushed brown hair away from a bruised, bite covered neck, and waited.

Simon rose with a swiftness characteristic of much older vampires and grabbed the girl around her throat. "I apologize, Rune. This one has only the bite on her mind, but she knows better than to—"

The girl gave a ragged, breathless screech, tore herself from Kelic's grip, and threw her underweight body at Rune. She ripped at her own neck with her nails, drawing blood, perhaps hoping the scent would entice Rune to have a taste.

Rune was not tempted—not even a little bit. "Get off me." She kept her voice calm, but the girl was starting to piss her off.

"Do it," the girl said. "Take a taste. Just one."

And as Rune started to give her a shove that would have sent her into the wall, the bite junkie pressed her bloody fingers to Rune's lips. "One taste. I can be yours. I don't like it here."

Simon growled and yanked her away from Rune. "Cherise," he said. He didn't raise his voice, but an older woman—likely Cherise—appeared at once. "Get rid of her."

Cherise dragged the pleading girl from the room.

Simon shook his head and closed his eyes for a long moment.

"They don't fear you," Rune said.

"I am reluctant to abuse the humans, even the bite junkies your humans care nothing about." He pulled a clean handkerchief from a small box beside her chair and offered it to her. He watched as she wiped her mouth.

She lifted an eyebrow. "That's because your brain is still human. That'll change with time."

Simon smiled. "Touché."

"Tell me about your vampire."

"She started feeling unwell three weeks ago. The blemishes appeared shortly after. Two nights ago, she projectile vomited all the blood she'd ingested for breakfast. It was the last meal she was able to consume."

"That's…" She shook her head and stuffed the handkerchief into her pocket.

He nodded. "She will be gone before long. Likely a couple of weeks if we don't find a cure."

"Is she the only one affected?"

He opened his mouth twice before he was able to get the words out. "Iker became sick this morning."

Simon's grief was unmistakable. His favorite was dying. *Shit.* "He looked fine," she said. "He *seemed* fine."

"I made him," the master said. "I know when he's unwell. I smell Anna's sickness on him. He will show signs soon. Soon, he will know." For a moment, he stared woodenly at the wall.

"What can I do?" she asked. She had to do something. If the vampires were infecting each other…or worse, if they infected the humans, the vampires would have to be destroyed.

"I don't know. I don't know what anyone can do." He looked at her, and his normally calm eyes were full of dark anguish. "But you have to help me. This will wipe us out. If the humans find out—"

"Your coven will be purged." And fuck if she wasn't sick of purging vampires. "I'll take this to the Annex, Simon. I have no choice. Eugene Parish is a friend of the Others. He has the resources to help."

"No. It doesn't appear to be affecting humans—only Others. But panic will spread and it will be…chaotic."

"It'll be a fucking free for all. I know. But—"

"If we go to ground, Rune, you will not find us."

"Don't run. I won't let him kill you. If he wants to purge, I'll warn you first. Then you can hide out somewhere close until we get this shit figured out."

He hesitated.

"Don't *run,* Simon," she said, her voice hard. "You'll end up destroying the entire vampire world if you do."

"If you don't help us find a cure, we're already destroyed."

"I will help. I'll do everything I can."

"Then swear it." He put a hand on her arm. "Give me your word we will not be destroyed by the Annex, and I'll trust you."

She opened her mouth, but the words wouldn't come. Dammit. She was getting soft. "I'll do my best. But I can only swear that I'll give you warning first, so you can hide. But if you do, don't go far. The Annex can find a cure."

She was sure of Eugene's willingness to help. Why would he go through the trouble of chasing and purging vampires who, without his help, were dead anyway?

She started to leave but stopped at the doorway. "More of them are sick, aren't they?"

Slowly, he nodded. "A dozen of them so far."

"How are you getting the infection?"

"I believe the humans we bite are carriers. They are passing it to us."

"We'll need to test a couple of your humans." She hesitated. "And your sick vampires, as well. I'll let you choose which ones to bring in."

She left him there, standing with his solemn face and hopeless future, and ran home to her own coven—her crew.

She ran home to Strad Matheson.

The berserker had become as much a part of her life as…feeding. And she needed him, whether she wanted to admit it out loud or not, just as badly.

He was waiting for her, standing still and watchful in the thick shadows of her porch.

She didn't see him, not at first, but she felt him.

"God, Strad," she murmured, and walked into his arms.

"What happened?" His voice rumbled into the night, dark and deep and strong.

The tightness inside her started to ease immediately.

She rubbed her cheek against his warmth, inhaling his familiar scent.

"Rune," he said. "What the fuck happened?"

She sighed and pulled grudgingly away. "I'm okay. But the vampires are sick. They're infected by something that's causing them to rot from the inside. It's spreading through Kelic's coven."

He nodded. "We'll have to purge them."

"No, Berserker. Eugene is not…"

Jeremy. Eugene is not Jeremy.

"He's not," Strad agreed. "But he'll want them contained."

"They'll die anyway if he doesn't help them. The Annex is pro-Other. He'll help. Kelic said the humans aren't getting infected—only the vampires."

"How are they infecting each other?"

"The humans are carriers. When the vampires feed from them, they get the disease." She shrugged. "At least that's what Simon believes."

"And how are these humans becoming carriers?"

"I have no idea. Eugene will have to test some samples. He'll figure out what's making them sick."

His stare was steady, but held something she did not like.

She didn't like it at all.

"All Others or just the vampires?" he asked.

"I'll find out tomorrow. I don't know anything other than what Simon told me, but this…" she stopped and put a hand to her chest. A vivid image of the bite junkie smearing blood across her lips slammed suddenly into her brain. "Oh."

Strad closed his eyes.

"You already had the thought, didn't you?" she whispered.

Why did she always forget she was a vampire?

Or...sort of a vampire.

He nodded, but said nothing. He looked at her, his eyes full of torment and resignation.

She shoved him hard enough to move him back. "*Fuck* you."

"Sweetheart." He rubbed his face, then crossed his arms. He didn't look at her, perhaps unwilling for her to see in his eyes that he'd already given her up for...

"I can't die," she said.

He knotted his jaws.

"I can't *die*, Berserker."

There were many things worse than death, but she couldn't think of one that would be worse than going through life rotting into a puddle of putrid jelly.

Brain in a jar.

She clutched her stomach. "God!"

He dragged her to him then, ignoring her resistance, and wrapped her in his arms. For an instant, he wiped out thoughts of the horror to come.

But only for an instant.

"No sign of Gunnar?" He squeezed her, hard.

She knew he was trying to help, knew he was trying to get her thoughts on something a little less horrifying.

"No. He's gone." She flinched at the unintentional sound of pain in her words.

Rot. Black, fucking rot.

But she might not even be infected. She could be immune.

So she pushed that worry deep into her mind and hid it beneath piles of other horrors.

She had to.

"He'll come back," the berserker said.

"Yeah. He'll come back and you'll find the little black-haired baby the Shop took."

He said nothing, and the silence drew out, long and prickly. At least it seemed that way to her.

But she wouldn't apologize to him for the words. She'd apologize if he found the baby. She'd apologize if the ghoul returned.

Until then, the berserker was out of luck.

And when her cell rang and she saw Elizabeth's number on the display, she was pretty sure he wasn't the only one.

CHAPTER THREE

"Elizabeth," Rune said. "Is it Fie?"

"Rune." Elizabeth's voice was tired and somehow confused.

Rune clutched her stomach with her free hand, drawing Strad's sharp stare. He took her hand, and she didn't draw away. Sudden fear spiked through her, and she knew she was about to hear something she really didn't want to hear.

"*Fuck*, Elizabeth," she murmured. "What is it?"

"Come in," Elizabeth said. "Just come in."

Gooseflesh arose on Rune's skin, and she shuddered with reaction—reaction to what, she couldn't have said—as she pushed her phone into her pocket.

"Rune," Strad said. He stood with a stillness that let her know he was ready to kill someone—she just had to say the word.

"Something's wrong with Fie," she told him.

"I'll drive," he said, and didn't seem surprised when she acquiesced. He knew from looking at her that she just wanted to huddle in a corner and weep.

"What the fuck is it?" he asked, as he drove too fast toward the Annex.

"I don't know. But it's something bad."

And when wasn't it? When *wasn't* it something bad?

"You're not completely healed."

"I'm healed, Berserker. I'm just…" What? Weaker?

More afraid? Her decapitation had kicked her ass.

She lifted her fingers to her throat and caressed the ridged scar, and a vivid image of black and red swirling chaos shot through her mind.

Whatever had happened after her near death—her *death*—had broken her in ways she'd never been broken.

Had made her different.

And as the days went by, images of something she couldn't quite grasp fluttered on the edge of her mind.

It left not a picture, but a feeling.

A feeling of something so overwhelming it took her breath.

Z.

Something…something Z.

And it had happened when she'd been lying in the Annex, trying to repair a severed head and a shredded heart.

What had she done?

She shook her head hard, trying to drive out the agonizing, furtive thought of something she couldn't grab onto.

"Rune?" The berserker reached across the seat and took her hand.

"I'm okay. I'm okay."

"Yeah. You are."

But neither one of them believed it.

It took an eternity to reach the Annex.

They strode into the building and down the corridor toward Fie's room, fear swirling so thick it was almost visible. They both loved the tiny necromancer.

She'd gone to hell and had never entirely returned. And she was just a child. Just a fucking baby.

Rune ran into the room, fully expecting to see the little girl lying still and unbreathing, encased in the netting that had taken over her body.

The netting had gradually closed and changed to resemble, as Elizabeth had said, a mud dauber's nest. It had climbed slowly until it covered her throat, her face, her head.

And there she had lain, locked within that horrible shell.

But no longer.

Elizabeth was standing at Fie's bedside. Eugene Parish stood at the other side, his eyes jumping with excitement.

"Rune," Elizabeth cried. "I...*look* at her."

Rune walked to the foot of the bed, and she looked.

Strad stood at her back and never made a sound.

Stefanie had changed.

"Hi, Rune," she said. "I got out."

Her voice was nasally and her words were not as clear as they'd once been, but Rune understood her.

"Yes," Rune said, breathless. "You did, sweetheart."

The little girl looked past Rune to the berserker. She held out her arms. "Pick me up."

Eugene rubbed his hands together. "We'll grow her some skin. Just as we did for you, Rune. Until then, a mask can be custom made—"

"Quiet," Elizabeth hissed. "You will be quiet!"

Fie glanced at her foster mother, but was only interested for a second in Elizabeth's distress. "Uncle B'serk," she said. "Pick me up."

"No, Stefanie," Elizabeth said, her voice gentle.

Strad strode to the side of the bed and nudged Elizabeth out of the way. "I'm holding her."

"She could get...she..." Elizabeth pushed her hair off her forehead with a shaking hand, unable to find the words. "You can't move her."

But he was the berserker, and he could do anything he wanted. He leaned over and scooped the child, blankets and all, into his arms.

He didn't look at anyone. Not even Rune.

"How long has she been free of the net?" Rune asked.

Elizabeth glanced at her watch. "Two hours. She wouldn't eat or drink. The techs drew blood."

"We'll know more when we have a look at her labs," Eugene said. He stood quietly, his stare never leaving the child.

Fie wiggled against Strad's chest. "Ow. You got too many hard things on."

He went pale. "Are you okay?"

"Uh huh. Can I go outside?"

Fie needed the outdoors. She needed the air, no matter how chilly. She'd spent a lot of time trapped inside the hell of the mysterious net.

Rune shuddered. She'd have gone stark raving mad. She took a deep breath. "Let's take her outside, Strad."

He nodded and headed for the door, ignoring Elizabeth's orders not to leave the room.

Rune put a hand on Elizabeth's arm and opened her mouth to reassure the woman, but before she could get a word out, Fie saw herself in the reflective glass of the door.

She gave a small scream, almost hidden by the berserker's curses as he realized the mistake he'd made.

He turned quickly and shielded the child from her reflection, but she struggled in his arms.

"Don't," she cried. "Let me see."

Strad looked at Rune for help.

"Let her see," Rune said. "Take her back, Berserker."

And no one argued.

It was time to let the child come face to face with her monster.

CHAPTER FOUR

Fie stared at her image without moving. Just stared.

At last, she tilted her head, then lifted her fingers to her face. She watched as the child in the mirror made the exact same movements.

"That's me?" she asked. "Am I scary?"

Elizabeth rushed to her. "No, darling. You're beautiful."

"Rune," Fie ordered.

"Yeah?"

"Am I scary?"

Rune sighed. "Yeah, baby. You're a little scary."

Fie continued looking in the mirror, turning her face from side to side, trying to purse lips that were just barely there. Watching, fascinated, the little girl with the fleshless face.

Then she grew bored. "Can we go outside now?"

Strad, still a little too pale, opened his mouth, then closed it. He cleared his throat. "What's happening?"

Rune grinned. "She's a kid."

"Wait," Fie cried, as Strad started once more for the door. "I want my pink hair bow. Put it in."

And once Elizabeth fastened the bow into her hair, the little girl was satisfied.

"You're beautiful," Elizabeth said.

"I know," Fie answered.

The net that had sheathed her hadn't appeared to touch her body. Her hands, her feet, the pale strip of her little belly that showed beneath her white top…all normal.

But it had eaten her face.

Huge, hollow black eyes stared calmly above the gray-white protrusions of her cheekbones. Tiny little teeth were set in a permanent grin above a pointy chin.

Her lids were so transparent her eyes were still visible when she closed them. Thin, flesh-colored lips clung with stubborn insistence.

Her face was an almost incomprehensible mess of gleaming bone, strips and patches and networks of red, blue, and gray muscles, nerves, blood vessels, and…

Hideousness.

Her hair was silky and fine and shiny with its side part and its pink hair bow. And despite her raw, skeletal face, innocence shined from her like a beacon.

"You know what, kid?" Rune said. "You really are a little beauty."

"I *know*," Fie said.

"Rune," Eugene said. "When you have a minute."

She nodded. "You coming, Elizabeth?"

"No. I need to speak with Eugene. Don't keep her outside long. And *watch* her."

They understood. They weren't to allow her to call the dead.

As if they could stop her.

Then Elizabeth and Eugene hurried off, planning and plotting things they had no intention of sharing.

Likely, Rune figured, a way to make a new face for Stefanie.

Surprisingly few people stared.

None of them pointed.

That could have been because they were all Annex workers and had grown accustomed to seeing shocking things.

Or maybe it was because the man who held the child

glared at them all with the sort of challenge not one of them was willing to accept.

"I saw Nikolai," Fie said, suddenly.

Rune shivered as a sudden chill swept through her. "Nicolas?"

"*Nikolai*," Fie insisted, almost angrily. "He is sad and bad."

"And," she went on, when no one said anything, "Brasque. *He's* good. He talked to me."

"When?" Rune whispered, then cleared her throat and tried again. "When, Fie?"

"After I went away."

"When you were hanging in the net?" Strad asked.

"When I was in the net. I went away."

Rune rubbed her arms and glanced at Strad. He lifted his eyebrows, as lost as she was.

"Who is Nikolai? And Brasque?"

Fie met Rune's stare. "He's nice."

"Do you know where you went?" Because suddenly, Rune had to know. "Where did you go?" She put a hand on Strad's arm and pulled him to a standstill.

"With the dogs. There were good places and bad places. I was in the good place but bad things were coming. Brasque made me leave."

Strad looked at Rune. "Just a dream."

But Rune shook her head. No. It was more than that. She could feel it like some sort of...*echo* coming from Fie's body. "It wasn't a dream, Berserker."

They took Fie outside, just past the sliding double doors. As soon as the air hit her skin, the tiny girl threw back her head and took a deep breath.

"Cold," she said, her voice lit with pleasure.

"Does it hurt your face?" Rune asked.

Fie didn't answer.

Where did you go, Fie? Where the fuck did you go?

Rune's cell rang, and she walked a few steps away to answer it. "Kelic. What is it?"

"You asked me if all Others were getting sick. I didn't have an answer. I do now."

She rubbed the bridge of her nose. "Fuck me."

"Yes. The infection does not discriminate. All Others are fair game." He hesitated. "Rune…"

"I'm already aware I may be infected, Kelic. If I find out that girl attacked me under your orders, the infection won't have a chance to get to you. Not before I do."

"I swear to you—"

"Save it," she said and clicked off.

Fie was falling asleep in the berserker's arms before she'd allow them to take her back to her room.

Elizabeth tucked her in, her brow knit with worry. "She'll be fine," she said to no one. And no one replied.

Rune leaned over the child to kiss her forehead. "See you soon, kid."

Fie shot open her thinly covered eyes and grabbed Rune's hair, wrapping it around her little fist. "They're waiting for you," she murmured. "To save them."

"Where, baby?"

"Where I went. Brasque said it's time for you to come there."

"I…" Rune had no idea what to say. She could barely speak past the taste of fear on her tongue.

"Rune," Fie hissed. "Take me with you. When you go, you take me with you. It's where I belong, too."

Strad jerked Rune away from the child, as though the kid might somehow carry her away to another world right then. "She's not going anywhere," he growled, "and neither are you."

And Fie began to cry, frightened by his tone.

Or maybe she was just disappointed by his words.

CHAPTER FIVE

She walked to Eugene's office as dawn broke, nothing but a low humming sound in her exhausted mind. She'd been working a lot of nights—not because she wanted to, but because that was just the way things had been happening.

Working at night, sleeping for a couple hours during the day before she was called out on another job. It wasn't anything she couldn't handle.

But the thought of rotting and Fie's horrible physical changes—as well as her chilling, portentous words—were pushing her toward the edge. Maybe the berserker was right. Maybe she wasn't completely healed.

Because she was fucking *tired*.

She pushed her palm against her stomach, wondering if she felt too much give there. Maybe the rotting had already started.

Shit.

"Rune," Eugene said, motioning her into his office. Then he frowned. "Are you ill?"

She realized right then that she wasn't ready to bring him in on the Other sickness. She just wasn't. She'd talk to him about it the next day, or the day after.

She dropped into the chair in front of his massive desk. "I'm fine."

He studied her for a moment longer. "Would you like

some coffee?"

"Let's talk about Bill Rice. That's why you wanted to see me, isn't it?"

He nodded, slowly, then focused on her words. "Yes. Bill. You've been working—perhaps too much. Are you feeling up to checking into Bill's circumstances?"

Eugene had noticed something off with Bill Rice weeks ago and had convinced her that spying on Bill would be a good idea. Maybe he was in trouble and too proud to ask for help.

Whatever was going on, she'd promised to check into it—then she'd gotten…sidetracked.

Being decapitated could put a girl behind schedule.

"I said I would. Where is he now?"

"I sent him to check into a situation in Dormer." He glanced at his watch. "He'll be back in a few hours. I'll text you when he gets back into town."

"All right. I'll tail him tonight."

Bill went nowhere but home that night. She stood outside his apartment, waiting to see if he'd leave again, but gave up after two hours. She'd follow him to keep him out of trouble, but she wasn't standing outside his house all fucking night.

She texted Eugene the information and decided, as she did every night, to check Wormwood for Gunnar.

Just in case.

It was just a little after midnight. If nothing unexpected happened, she might actually be able to go home and finish off the night in her bed.

With the berserker.

She jogged to her car, checked the glove box for Baby Ruth candy bars, and then headed for Wormwood.

She took a deep breath and caressed the decapitation scars on her throat, unable to shake the feeling of heavy depression that squeezed her brain.

Something was coming.

Or maybe it was already there.

"Gunnar," she muttered, somewhat comforted by the sound of her voice. "I'm just worried about that crazy fucking ghoul."

Yeah. That's what it was.

She wandered Wormwood aimlessly, then finally placed the candy on a large rock and walked away from the graveyard. She hadn't even expected to find Gunnar.

She just wasn't a glass half full type of person.

Too unsettled to go home, she drove into the city, left her car in the lot of an open all night grocery chain, and began to run.

Fast.

Her speed was crazy. She missed a lot while shooting through the air like a wayward bullet, but she worked off some excess energy. Some fear.

She saw things as she raced by—two women fighting, a man stabbing a tree and screaming, and when she neared Willowburg, a car with its engine running, lights on, one door open. No one inside.

She should have investigated, perhaps, all those things.

But she didn't. She turned back toward Spiritgrove, a little slower, her mind slightly less anxious.

She'd been through shit before. Bad shit. And she always came back. Always triumphed over the pain.

She'd be okay.

So she ran through the night, suddenly eager to reach home. The twins and Lex and Ellie were there.

The berserker was there.

She took a different route back to her car. She came up behind the grocery, thinking about Strad, and Owen, and Z…

Always Z.

And she ran right past the dead man nailed to the building before her mind grabbed on to what her eyes had seen.

"Son of a bitch," she murmured.

River County's serial killer had been quiet for a while.

She'd begun to believe he'd moved on to other hunting grounds.

She'd been wrong.

The victim had been slashed so brutally he was almost too shredded to identify as human, or male, or anything other than bloody meat.

She pulled her cell from her pocket and told the Annex night duty to send the lab. She left Bill a voicemail because he didn't answer his phone, then called Eugene.

"Where are you?" she asked.

"I'm home for once. I hope this is not something someone else could have handled."

She lifted an eyebrow. Eugene wasn't often cranky. "Bill didn't answer his phone, so I called you. I found a body nailed to the back of Garvey's Grocery."

"Our guy?"

"Yes."

He cursed under his breath. "Call the Annex and have—"

"Already did. I was just giving you a heads up."

"Next time, phone Elizabeth first. She'll know whether or not it's worth disturbing me." He hung up.

"Asshole," she muttered, and pulled her keys from her pocket. There was a penlight attached, and she used it to study the victim.

He was the same as the others. Brutalized, killed, nailed.

Their killer was one angry dude.

She called Bill again. The serial killer was his baby, and no one was more interested than he was.

Finally, he answered, his voice groggy and thick.

"Dammit, Bill," she said. "Since when don't you answer your phone?"

"I just did, didn't I?" he growled.

She took her phone away from her ear to stare at it for a long moment. "What the fuck is up with everybody tonight?" she asked.

"Rune." He cleared his throat, and she heard him take a long drink of something. "I apologize. What happened?"

"Your serial killer happened. I just found another body."

"Where?" His voice was sharper, more alert.

"Garvey's Grocery." She hesitated, then, "Are you okay, Bill?"

"Yeah, I'm fine." But his words were too stilted, too overly casual. "Why do you ask?"

"I don't know," she lied. "The whole city is fucked up tonight."

"I'll be there in half an hour. Go home, get some rest." Then it was his turn to pause. "Be with your people, Rune."

He didn't say it, but the unspoken words echoed in her mind.

Be with your people, Rune.
While you still can.

CHAPTER SIX

The house was silent when she got home, silent except for Lex, who wasn't the best sleeper. She wandered the house, her steps light and quick, despite the darkness. But then, Lex lived in darkness.

The others were asleep, she supposed. If they'd gotten called out she hadn't been notified, so most likely they hadn't been called out.

The berserker was in her bed.

She undressed quickly and climbed in with him, shivering as he pulled her against his solid warmth.

"Okay?" he asked.

"Yeah."

"Hungry?"

She smiled against his chest, then darted out her tongue to taste his smooth flesh. "Yeah."

He ran his hand over her back, saying nothing.

But she knew he was hungry, too.

"Berserker."

"Yes."

"The month I was out of commission…"

"What about it?"

"Did you try to get my bite?"

His hand went still and he stiffened. "Rune."

She shrugged. "The addiction is a bad son of a bitch. Not many could have resisted."

"You don't trust me."

She swallowed. "I'd trust you with my life."

"Your life doesn't mean much to you."

She heard the pain in his voice and closed her eyes. "I care about my life more than I used to, Berserker. I don't care for my immortality."

"You didn't ask if the twins or Lex tried to feed."

"I…" Dammit. No, she hadn't.

"Fucking addiction." His voice was hoarse. Harsh.

So despairing.

She didn't ask him how she was supposed to trust a man whose addiction would shatter anything but his need. His addiction was her fault. He'd become addicted by saving her life.

She owed him.

But that didn't mean she had to completely trust him.

Not with her heart.

That was going to take a while.

He pushed her to her back and loomed over her, his long hair sliding over his shoulders. "Talking about it won't change things. I'll fix it, Rune."

But they both knew the addiction wasn't fixable.

"You said you love me."

"Yeah?"

She shook her head. "Why? If not for the addiction, why?"

Owen's words echoed in her mind. *"You're hot, you're a freak, and I dig you…"*

Strad stared down at her for a long, breathless moment. Then, he smiled. He kissed her lips, gently. "Because you're the best person I've ever known. Because when I'm not with you, I need to be. Because from the beginning, I wanted you. Because no matter what the reasons, being with you is the only time I'm…" He paused, then lifted his fist to hit his chest. "The only time I'm not the berserker."

She wasn't sure if his words made it better, or worse.

She put her palms on either side of his face and pulled

him to her, reveling in the taste of his lips, his vitality.

She knew what he meant.

It was the same way for her. When she was with him, like that, in bed, in darkness, alone…she was peaceful.

Quiet.

"Oh," she whispered, pulling away. "You're how I find the silence?"

She didn't know what that might mean. She only knew it was the truth.

She'd come far, and she ended up finding the silence in the berserker's fucking arms.

Whatever that meant.

And yeah, it was crazy. They were both too messed up to find peace with each other. Weren't they?

"Whatever," she said. "Fuck it."

"Yeah," he agreed. "Fuck it."

But his sorrow was as thick as syrup. Thick enough to taste.

She ran her hands over his massive shoulders and down his back. There was only ever that one moment.

Whatever else that came would come.

It really was out of her control.

"I *am* yours, Rune," he said.

"I know. And I'm your addiction."

"I'll prove myself to you." Then, he hesitated. "I'm stronger than my addiction. I'm stronger than your bite."

"I almost believe you," she said. "But we both know—"

"Be quiet," he said, softly. Tenderly.

"Make me," she answered, smiling.

So he did.

What woke her up four hours later wasn't anything out of the ordinary—screams in her dream. Someone was always screaming her dreams.

But when she startled awake, her heart beating with chunky, painful irregularity against her damaged chest, the screams continued.

They were real.

Screams of laughter.

Evil. Wicked.

Doom.

I know you.

How did I forget?

She leaped from the bed, only then realizing the berserker was not beside her. She shot out her claws and raced into the living room, almost knocking Lex over in her rush.

"What the fuck is it?" she asked. "Who is it?"

But she knew.

Levi and Denim ran into the room, half-dressed, wild-eyed, blades ready.

Ellis peeped around the corner, a hand to his chest.

The screams of laughter reverberated off the walls, strident and mind-numbing. Horrifying.

And no one was there.

The crew stood back to back, circling slowly, ready to fight an enemy they could not see.

"What is it?" Ellis cried.

"Stay put, Ellis," Levi ordered.

"But what *is* it?"

"Better question," Denim said. "Where is it?"

Rune probed the ceiling with her narrowed gaze, then glanced at Lex. "Lex," she said, quietly, "what are you getting?"

"Oh, Rune," Lex whimpered. "Oh, Rune."

Rune withdrew her claws and yanked Lex to her. "What the fuck is it?"

Lex, her crazy eyes dancing, put her palms over her ears. "She has something that belongs to you. Oh it's…no. She has your blood." Then—

"Where's Strad? Ah…" She drooled, which scared Rune more than her words had. Until they sunk in.

She let go of Lex, threw back her head, and screamed at the ceiling. *"Berserker!"*

Lex fell to the floor, and Ellis shot into the room. He grabbed her collar and dragged her into the hallway.

"Berserker," Rune screamed, again.

Maybe she was still dreaming. Maybe she was asleep. Maybe…

"Rune," Levi said, grabbing her shoulders and shaking her. "The berserker doesn't fucking *laugh*."

She began shivering and was unable to stop. Her teeth chattered as she tried to get the words out. "No. But Damascus does. And Strad…"

"What, Rune?"

"Strad is gone," she whispered.

And Rune needed her fucking berserker.

CHAPTER SEVEN

Strad had left her a text message after he'd slipped from her bed.

I'll be back.

That was all.

She called his phone a dozen times, but got no answer.

So she paced, furious. Helpless.

Neither Eugene nor the Annex had contacted him. She'd called to check.

"What does that bitch want?" she muttered, pacing back and forth, her fists clenched. "Blood? What does that mean?"

"Maybe she's building her own monsters," Denim murmured.

She stopped abruptly. "Shit."

"What is it?" Owen asked.

Ellis had called the rest of the crew in, and all of them sat or stood in her kitchen, waiting for some concrete orders. Something they could do.

All but Jack. He hadn't answered Ellis's summons.

"Fie told me she went away when she was trapped in the net. She said I belonged there. She went to Damascus's world—I know it." She grabbed her jacket off the back of a kitchen chair. "I have to talk to her. Something is waiting there."

"Rune!" Ellis grabbed her arm. "You can't want to go

there. You can't. No matter what anyone says, *this* is where you belong."

"Maybe it is, Ellie, but that cunt is making herself known for a reason. If she's going to keep messing with us, I might belong there for just a little while." Her smile stretched her face, and she knew when Ellie backed away, his eyes wide, that it wasn't a nice smile.

She didn't give a fuck. She had to meet the threat head on. She had to chase it, catch it, and beat it to a bloody pulp.

Because she was scared, so scared, and she'd be damned if she'd let that fear control her.

If the witch wanted her, she was eventually going to find a way to get her.

And if that happened, Rune was going to make her regret it.

"I have no idea how to get there," she muttered. And she realized when relief touched her that a big part of her really, really didn't want to figure it out.

"You know how," Lex said, her voice dull, her eyes sluggish.

She'd had some kind of seizure when the laughter had pinged off the walls of the house, and coming out of it had been a long, hard process.

Rune knelt down beside her chair. "How, Lex? Reverence? Orson's house?"

"No. Not Reverence."

"Where?"

Lex sighed, the breath floating from her lips hot and thick and smelling of wood smoke.

Rune didn't understand her reluctance, and she didn't care what caused it. "Lex. Where?"

"Wormwood," Lex whispered, finally. The words hung in the air, ominous and heavy.

Rune nodded and got to her feet. It was a start. "First Fie, then the graveyard. Maybe I'll find that fucking ghoul while I'm at it."

And though her words were cool and a little flippant, not one person in that room would have been fooled by her tone.

Rune was hurting, and they knew it.

She grabbed her phone and keys off the kitchen table. "Where the fuck is Jack," she muttered, and punched in his number for the sixth time.

"We're going to take care of Annex business," Raze said. "You do what you need to do." When she didn't acknowledge his words he clasped her shoulder. "Rune."

"Yeah?" she looked at him, a little dazed. "What?"

"You call us when you need us. Don't go anywhere without your crew."

She took a deep breath, then nodded. "I wouldn't think of it."

She left them there and went to her car, unsurprised when Lex got into the passenger seat.

"I'm swinging by Jack's before I go to see Fie," Rune told her.

"Yeah." Lex hesitated. "It'll be okay, Rune."

"I know." Rune glanced at her, relieved the little Other seemed better. Stronger.

"If you go there," Lex said, "you'll be doing exactly what she wants you to do."

"No," Rune disagreed. "If I go there, it'll be because I have no choice. And when I get there…" She silently cursed the fear that rose up to choke her at the thought. "It's time that bitch ends. And I'm going to be the one to end her."

Lex turned to stare sightlessly out her window, silent.

Jack, Fie, Wormwood.

Strad.

She kept that string of words flowing through her head all the way to Jack's house. It was the only thing that kept her from shattering into a million pieces.

Jack lived in a tiny bungalow on a quiet street in the city, and when she pulled into his driveway, she realized she'd only been to his house twice since she'd known him.

The first time he'd met her in his yard, and the second time he stood at the door and hadn't asked her in.

But when he didn't answer her hard knock, she didn't care that he might not want people inside his house.

She kicked the door, just hard enough to force it open, but not hard enough to destroy it.

She had a little restraint, despite the nervous energy begging her to let it out.

"Jack," she bellowed. "Where the fuck are you?"

Maybe he's dead.

Shit. Stop being a paranoid little bitch.

"Jack," she yelled again, her mind noticing—and filing away for later—the dark emptiness of his living room. She charged down a skinny hall, pushing open the first door she came to. There were only two. The second one likely contained a bathroom, because the first one was Jack's bedroom.

"God," she said, putting her hand to her nose.

The room stank of whiskey, vomit, and mustiness.

It smelled lonely and sad.

Just a little fucking sad.

She flipped his light on and stared around the room, shocked. "Shit, Jack."

He looked like he'd just fallen across his mattress in a drunken stupor. His legs hung off the bed, and he still wore his boots and jeans.

The room contained only the bed and a dresser. The walls were bare. And though the room was neat, he'd flung his shirt to the floor, half covering some empty whiskey bottles.

And his eye patch.

She closed her eyes as pity reached out a relentless hand to choke her.

It was good Lex had waited in the car. No one needed to see him like that.

The bed dipped as she sat down beside his still form.

She took the empty whiskey bottle from his lax fingers and placed it on the floor, then slipped her hand into his.

"Jack," she murmured. "Wake up, baby."

He didn't stir.

After a couple of minutes she got up, found the bathroom, and filled a glass with cold water. She carried it back to the bed and without hesitating, tossed the water onto his face.

He came off the bed roaring, his hands reaching for weapons that weren't there.

She stood back against the wall and waited.

He focused on her finally.

"Fuck you, Rune," he said, his voice hoarse. "Get the fuck out of here."

She walked to him and wrapped her arms around his body. She pressed her cheek against his flesh and again, she waited.

At last, he sighed and hugged her to him. "How bad is it?"

"It's bad, Jack," she said. "It's pretty fucking bad."

And they stood there in each other's arms until Lex sounded the horn, urging them to action.

CHAPTER EIGHT

"I don't care about Bill fucking Rice," Rune said, pacing Eugene's office.

"And I know you don't mean that," Eugene said, watching her.

Rune rubbed the bridge of her nose. "The berserker is missing. The ghoul is missing. Fie is missing her face. And…"

"What is it?"

She blew out a hard breath. "Call in Elizabeth and Bill. I don't want to have to repeat myself."

He didn't hesitate.

While Eugene was calling them in, she went into the hall to make a phone call.

She called a floater she trusted and asked him to go to Bill's house at night to watch for movement. If Bill left the house, or if anyone went into his house, the floater would call her.

She had too much to do to watch the house herself.

Bill and Elizabeth came in at the same time. They both looked tired, both looked worried. And Rune was about to add to it.

Without further delay, she told them about the Other sickness spreading through the town. "Right now it's quiet. That's going to change real fucking soon."

"How could I not have heard about this?" Eugene

picked up his phone, slammed it back down, and glared at her.

"Your sources are not my problem," she said. "What I need to know is if you're going to help. I'm not purging any vampires. The Others need your help. Are you going to give it to them?"

To us?

He stared her down. "I'd rather have a world full of Others than a world full of humans, Rune. Of course I'm going to help." He stood. "Now everybody out. I have to get to work on this before every fucking Other in the world is wiped out."

Rune didn't move. "Eugene, if you—"

He held up a hand. "Don't even think of threatening me. You'll just make me angry and waste time we don't have." He leaned over his desk, his eyes intense. "If you need me to give you a selfish reason, here it is. Without the Others, I'm no one. All this goes away."

He let her think about that for a second.

She nodded. "Okay."

He straightened, once again picking up his phone. "Now get out and let me do my job."

"Are you okay?" Elizabeth asked, once she, Rune, and Bill were outside Eugene's office. "Have you heard from Strad?"

"Not yet." And she wasn't going to pull out her phone to check again. Not with Elizabeth and Bill watching her.

"What can you tell us?" Bill asked.

Rune eyed him, noticing the scratches on his neck and the bruise high on his cheekbone. "He was in bed with me. I went to sleep, then woke up to…laughter. We couldn't see anyone, but I know it was Damascus." She shook her head. "Her voice came through loud and clear."

"Be careful, Rune. If she wants you there…"

Rune had to clear her throat before she could speak. "Fuck her."

"If there's anything I can do," Bill said, "let me know."

"I need to see Fie. Is she awake?"

Elizabeth glanced at her wrist, then realized she wasn't wearing a watch. "Yes. But please don't upset her."

Rune didn't bother replying. She probably would upset the kid, and Elizabeth knew that.

Bill hurried on down the hallway, passing up Fie's room without another word.

"What's wrong with him?" Rune asked Elizabeth. She toyed with the idea of telling the other woman that Bill was in trouble and that Eugene had asked her to spy on him, but decided against it.

She needed more information before she confided in Elizabeth.

"I don't know," Elizabeth answered. "He hasn't been himself for a while now."

And she was too involved with little Stefanie to care.

Bill was being neglected, really, by all of them.

She could only wait to hear something from the watching floater.

She wouldn't know what to do without an overflowing plate.

"Strad will be back, Rune."

Rune didn't miss a step. "I know." Of course he'd be back. His mind wouldn't survive without feeding his addiction. Not for long.

But *why* had he gone? Why?

And then she stopped walking, only marginally aware that Elizabeth was speaking to her.

No.

"I'll prove myself to you, Rune. I'm stronger than my addiction. I'm stronger than your blood."

"Oh, God."

"Rune?" Elizabeth frowned. "What is it?"

"He's going to prove himself."

"Who?"

"The berserker. He's going to prove he's stronger than the addiction."

He'd prove it, or he'd die.

And no one was stronger than her fucking blood and bite. No one.

Not even Strad Matheson.

"Oh, God," she said, again.

But she wouldn't let it break her heart.

She wouldn't.

So she got angry instead.

"I'll never leave you, Rune."

"Not even if I want you to?"

"Not even then."

Fucking liar.

She pushed her fist into her abdomen so hard it hurt.

It hurt so much.

He'd lied to her again.

Before she could lose herself in the misery of another betrayal, the nurse Elizabeth had left with Fie came running from the room.

"Thank goodness you're here," she said. "She's..." Then she shook her head and ran back into the room, Rune and Elizabeth at her heels.

Fie floated above the bed, her arms and head hanging. Her hair waved gently.

"Stefanie," Elizabeth cried, and ran to her side.

The child's eyes were rolled back, her mouth slack. She made no sounds. She looked eerily similar to the way Lex had looked when the witch's laughter had assaulted them.

Rune ripped her phone from her pocket.

"Lex," she said, when the girl answered. "I need you in Fie's room *now*."

"Impossible. I'm waiting for you outside Wormwood."

"What? How the hell did you get to Wormwood? Get your fucking demon on and fly your ass here, Lex. Do it *now*."

And she shook with the effort it took her not to call Lex's demon.

Because in that room, at that moment, she felt the

presence of Damascus.

She wasn't sure if she needed Lex so desperately because she believed Lex might be able to keep her there, or if she was secretly afraid she'd be snatched away without Lex.

Her demon.

Or maybe she just needed a hand to hold.

CHAPTER NINE

But Lex wasn't going to let anyone order her to become her demon.

By the time she arrived at the Annex, Fie was curled into a little ball on her bed, asleep.

Lex didn't apologize, and Rune didn't expect her to. She had nothing to apologize for. Her demon was her own.

Interrogating Fie was out of the question, so Rune pulled Lex back out into the hallway.

"I want you to stay away from Wormwood, Lex. That's an order." Because worse than the fear that she'd be taken was the fear that Lex would.

If Karin Love was there with Damascus, and if she had any say in it, Lex would be taken.

Lex shook her head, her braids flying, her eyes jerking. "No. If you try to sneak away someday I need to know where the portal is so I can follow. You're never going to survive there without me. You just won't."

"You can't come with me." Rune hesitated. "Your mother…"

"Yes, Karin Love might be there. And I proved I can handle that bitch." Then it was her turn to hesitate. "But don't let the twins get involved. *They* can't."

Shit. She didn't want to risk Lex. But…

"Back to Wormwood?" Lex asked.

"I don't know. Maybe."

"The portal is there, Rune. We just have to find it. I can get us in—I'm sure of it." She paused. "Pretty sure."

"Lex, I don't want to lose you." *And I don't want to go to that fucking world.*

She had a bad, bad feeling.

Chances were high that she wouldn't make it back.

Lex ignored her words. "He'll be back." She shot out her hand and wrapped her fingers around Rune's wrist. Then, "He's not lost to you."

Rune's stomach tightened. "I can't imagine a world without the berserker."

Lex hesitated, then blurted, "Some of the Others in the graveyard were sick."

Rune shuddered and pulled out of Lex's grip. "I know."

"Do you think—"

"I don't know. I don't know anything except Strad and Gunnar are missing and no matter what the fuck else happens…" But she didn't know what to say.

Lex nodded. She kept pace with Rune's frenzied stride all the way to the car, keeping whatever other thoughts she had to herself.

When they pulled up to the gates of Wormwood, Rune sat staring through the windshield at nothing. "I can't feel him anymore," she said. "I can't *feel* him."

Lex opened her car door and jumped out, then stuck her head back in to reply. "Let's get him back and you can feel him all you want."

"Yeah." Rune shook her head once, hard, and then grinned at the little Other. "Let's get him back."

Jack, the twins, Owen, and Raze all stood outside Wormwood. She shot out her claws as she walked toward them. She gave Raze a sharp glance. "You said you were going to take care of Annex business. What the hell are you doing here?"

"We know you, Rune. And we're not letting you do this

on your own." He looked at Lex. "Neither one of you."

She wasn't surprised. They were Shiv Crew, and they'd never once let her take on a job without them, no matter how risky it might be to them. "I'm not going anywhere—but I need to know where an entrance is. Just in case."

They didn't seem mollified.

"Watch out for sick Others, boys," she went on. "I don't know if their virus or infection or whatever the fuck it is makes them mean or just sick, but be careful."

"So what are we looking for?" Raze asked.

"Lex thinks the way to Damascus is in Wormwood. I have no idea what to look for."

"Don't you think we'd have seen it by now if the door or window or whatever the hell it is were here?" Levi asked. "If you chase this thing down, you'll be making a mistake, Rune."

She stopped just inside the gates and turned toward them. Searching for the portal would keep her mind off the berserker. And the rot that even then might have been growing inside her. "Maybe we should look for Strad as well."

She closed her eyes, wishing she could call the words back.

No one said a word.

"Fuck you," she said.

"Strad can take care of himself," Owen said, his voice bland. "If there's a battle he needs to fight, he'll fight it. Maybe he'll win it. And if he wants to, he'll find his way back. But Damascus. Even if she has your blood, or anything else, she's not worth risking you over."

"She can't come back to you," Levi said. "So she's trying to lure you there. Leave her be, Rune."

Denim stared down at her, his scar vivid against the paleness of his face. He said nothing, but he didn't have to.

She knew they all believed she would be foolish to risk herself. And them.

And for what?

God, I wish I knew.

But she felt it like a poison in her veins. She needed to go.

That need got stronger by the minute.

It had nothing to do with want. She didn't *want* to go.

"Besides," Jack said, adding his voice to other naysayers. "There are battles here for you to fight. Leave Damascus to her world and worry about your own."

But maybe that world *was* her own.

That was the pull. That was the need.

To find herself.

Maybe, to go home.

Just for a little while.

But the part of her that felt the call was finally choked and smothered and kicked away by the part of her that viewed Damascus and the other world with terror. She didn't want to leave the world she knew and those who loved her.

Those she loved.

No call was stronger than that.

Eventually she might be forced to go. But until then, she was staying the fuck put.

That decision made her feel a little better.

"Okay," she said, and she almost smiled at their surprise. "Let's get out of here. The Annex has some jobs for us."

"We *can* search for Strad," Lex offered.

Rune hesitated.

"No," Raze said. "He's on his own."

"You'd do it if any one of us went missing," Lex said. "You haven't accepted the berserker yet. Not completely. You still don't trust him."

"And you do?" Levi asked her.

The twins were not over Strad's part in their time on the mountain.

Lex nodded. "I do. The point is, he's crew. He's Shiv Crew. Unless he's kicked out, you need to give him everything you've got. You'd do it for me and I'm Karin Love's daughter."

Raze gazed at her, almost, but not quite smiling. Raze wasn't a smiler. "You've never given us reason not to trust you, girl. Strad Matheson has."

He was right.

"Let's fight for whatever we need to fight for," Jack said. "I say we leave Strad to his shit. But if he comes back and needs us, then we'll fight for the fucking berserker."

Before Rune could reply, Lex gasped and spun around. "He's here," she said.

Rune's heart leaped and she turned in a circle, trying to see what the blind Other saw. "Strad?"

"No," Lex replied. She stood still and pointed toward the trees. *"Gunnar."*

CHAPTER TEN

And he wasn't alone.

"Gunnar," Rune cried, forgetting, for one brief second, the witch, the berserker, and the rotting sickness.

She loped toward the ghoul, who stood like a skinny, dark sentinel just inside the tree line.

A woman stood with him.

"Gunnar," she said again, reaching him in seconds. She grabbed his thin shoulders and shook him a little too hard. "Damn you."

"Your Highness," he whispered.

Then she noticed his condition. She stopped shaking him and squeezed his shoulder. "Who has hurt you?" She dropped her fangs and looked at the woman with him.

"*I* didn't hurt him," the woman said, "and the only reason I'm not hurting you for laying hands on what's mine is because he asked me not to. Because I owe him my freedom, you live."

Rune stared. The woman was tall, blonde, and a ghoul. And obviously, she was either very stupid, or very powerful, with her careless threats and her cold gaze.

But Rune appreciated her loyalty.

"Who the fuck are you?" Rune asked, but immediately turned back to Gunnar. He'd returned. She really didn't care about the female ghoul.

"This is Dawn," Gunnar said, his voice weak. "She is

my…"

"I'm his everything," Dawn said, when Gunnar trailed off. "Which is why he brought me back."

Gunnar wouldn't meet Rune's eyes.

And that told her that Dawn was lying.

Or maybe she was simply misinformed.

The crew gathered at Rune's back.

"What happened to you, Gunnar?" Levi asked.

Lex shied away, unwilling to touch either ghoul.

Gunnar listed suddenly to the side, and Raze stepped in to catch him. The ghoul's emaciated arm nearly disappeared in Raze's huge fist.

"Lean on me," Raze told Gunnar, his voice growly and angry.

"*You* are a hero," Dawn said to Raze.

They all looked at her for a second, then dismissed her and put their attention back on Gunnar.

Gunnar would look only at Rune. "It was not my intention to worry you, or to be absent for so long. Or," he continued, glancing down almost sheepishly at his battered body, "to take so much damage."

Rune resisted the almost overwhelming urge to hug the wild-haired ghoul. "Tell me everything."

"That would be impossible," Dawn said. "He does not *know* everything."

Rune lifted an eyebrow at the strange female. When she looked back at Gunnar, she could have sworn he was blushing. Or he would have been, if he'd been human. "Gunnar," she prompted.

"I had to show you it was possible, Your Unbalancedness. I would not have you lose your faith when you fear all is lost." His gaze sharpened. "And you will."

Fuck me.

She couldn't breathe. His words and the knowledge in his eyes snatched the air out of her lungs and she could not *breathe*.

"God," she finally said. "I knew something was coming."

And once again, her body started to shake. Some part of her knew what he was saying, knew what he was warning her about.

She looked around, unaware that she searched instinctively for the berserker until Owen stepped up behind her and put his hands on her shoulders.

"Steady," he murmured.

"Damascus?" she asked, ignoring the wobble in her voice.

Dawn shrieked and covered her face.

Gunnar didn't even glance at her. "Yes. But not only Damascus."

"How do you know this?" Jack asked. "How the fuck can you know anything?"

"Because he's magic." Lex slid a little closer to Rune. "Just as Rune is."

"I retrieved Dawn from the clutches of all that is death," Gunnar said. "*Damascus*. In her world, she is stronger than you are, Rune. Much stronger. You can't become…" He frowned, struggling to find the right word. "Careless. You must not surrender."

"Never give up," Dawn said, peeking out at Rune from behind her fingers. "Be as I was. Keep a place inside your heart that knows the darkness will not last forever."

"I liberated her from Damascus," Gunnar said. "Though it took me a lifetime."

"I always knew you would," Dawn said, smiling at Gunnar.

Gunnar glanced at Rune, and then quickly away.

Rune smiled through the horror. "I am so glad you're back."

He tried to bow, and had it not been for Raze's grip, he would have toppled over. He righted himself, heartbreakingly earnest in his obvious regard for Rune. "I have been without treats for quite some time."

"If you're able to walk," she told him, "you'll find candy all over Wormwood. I brought some every night since you've been gone."

"He will recover," Dawn said, puffing out her chest, "with me to nurse him. I will take care of him, and I will retrieve his treats." She nodded at them. "Go away now."

"Not yet," Rune said. "Gunnar, are you saying I have to go there?"

"Fool," Dawn said.

"Rune," Levi said. "You can't—"

"Be silent," Gunnar said, so out of character the crew could only stare. "This is Rune's path to follow. She will follow it."

No one said a word.

"Listen to the echoes of Wormwood," Gunnar said. "Open yourself to them. When you hear them, follow the path. It was always meant for you, Rune."

"Lead me there, Gunnar," she said. "If the time comes I have no choice but to go, come with me."

"I cannot, Your Majesty. I would crumble into dust were I to attempt the journey again. But I have prepared them for you."

She frowned. "Who did you prepare?"

"Your allies, Rune. You will not be totally alone."

Then he motioned her to him, and leaned down to whisper quickly into her ear.

"The echoes of Wormwood are inside you. Listen. Prepare. It is time to heed them."

He seemed suddenly so human, so different, that she couldn't say anything.

But she understood.

Wormwood echoed.

She had only to listen.

And she was not fucking ready.

Because in her heart, she knew she might never come back.

CHAPTER ELEVEN

"If you find a way in, you have to let us go in with you. We're addicted," Denim said, later, standing outside the Annex. "Without you, we'll suffer until we die anyway."

Fuck if he wasn't right.

What could she do? Take them to almost certainly suffer and die, or leave them where they would unquestionably suffer and die, and maybe in an even worse way?

As Strad, alone in his addiction, would be suffering?

Berserker.

"We're the original Shiv Crew," Raze said, pointing at himself, then Jack. "There is nothing for us here. We belong at your side."

"I would *rather* die than be left behind," Ellis said, resolute. He'd been waiting outside the Annex doors when they'd arrived.

He squeezed the tiny bulge of the fang hidden beneath his shirt. "You're my best friend. You're my life. *Levi* is my life." He released a quick sob. "The crew is my life."

Owen shrugged. "I just like to travel." He grinned at her.

But his eyes were dead serious.

Not one of her crew was willing to let her go running off to some other world alone, even though none of them believed she should go. And despite her fear that they'd die there, that she would be taking them into a Damascus-laden trap, she nodded.

She needed her crew.

Her friends.

So she nodded.

"Okay then," Jack said. "Now how do we get there?"

"You heard Gunnar," she said, walking with her crew into the building.

"Yeah, but he made no sense. Echoes? Paths? I need something I can see and feel. I can't grab hold of some echoing shit."

"Not you," Lex said. "Rune. And she'll lead you there. *We* will lead you there. Exactly like when we walked through hell to get to the lab."

"I have a feeling that was a sweet little stroll over a pretty pink bridge," Jack said, "compared with what we'll face this time."

Rune agreed. "If I'm not snatched up by the witch and taken there, we're all staying put. I'm not losing you because Damascus is calling."

Lex grabbed her arm and pulled her around. "Don't enter Wormwood without us."

"I won't go there without any of you, Lex." She put her hand over Lex's.

She felt anxiety coming from all of them. They weren't worried about what was waiting for them once they left their world. They were worried she'd go without them. She looked around at them. "If I'm forced to go, and if it's within my power, you are going with me."

"Then don't take any chances," Levi said. "Stay out of Wormwood until we're all with you."

"I won't go into Wormwood without you," she repeated.

She explained to Eugene, Bill, and Elizabeth exactly what was happening. Neither Bill nor Elizabeth argued when she told them she might suddenly disappear to go fight a personal battle in...wherever the hell Damascus was.

Maybe they just didn't believe her.

Eugene, though, was not happy. "Your first duty is to this city, Rune. When I call, I expect you to come."

"If I'm not in another world," she said, dryly, "I will do my job here."

And she would.

Fucking echoes.

Maybe she'd been hearing them all her life, but hadn't understood what they were.

She was pretty sure that when she heard them, now that she knew to listen, the sounds would be as familiar to her as the constant sensations of her pain.

"Any updates about the Other sickness?" she asked him.

He steepled his fingers and sighed. "Not yet. I have two of the master's bite junkies and two sick vampires. Once the infection is isolated, we'll know more. I have to find out who cooked it up, and you know I'm going to need you here to help with that."

She frowned. "You think someone deliberately created it to destroy Others?"

He lifted an eyebrow. "There are no naturally occurring viruses that Others can contract, Rune. You don't get sick like humans. Of course this one is lab created. And it's bad."

When he said *"You"* instead of *"they,"* she took a second to acknowledge the fact that she only felt a tiny twinge of humiliation. And that was simply from habit.

She'd accepted her monster.

I am my monster.

And I'm proud of the little bastard.

"What's funny, Rune?"

"Sorry?"

"You were smiling."

"Nothing. How fast can your people create a cure?"

"I doubt they can. But they'll work on an antidote—Others not yet sick will be able to get inoculated against this virus, we hope."

"Like a flu shot."

"Yes. Like that."

"The ones already sick?"

He shook his head. "I don't know if we can help them. At least not in time. We're working on it but it's going to take time. Rune…"

"I don't know if I'm sick. I don't know."

He nodded. "I'm sorry."

"If the vampires can't feed from humans, they will die."

"And if they feed from infected humans, they will die."

They studied each other for a long moment. "What's going to happen, Eugene?"

"It's too early. I don't know."

She got up. "Who do you think created it? The Shop? COS?"

He stared up at her for a long, long moment. "I think it was the Next."

She narrowed her eyes. "Why?"

"I'm not completely sure, but it's…" He stood as well and began to pace, his fists clenched. "They're the only group I can think of that might be capable of this particular nasty. I have to fix this," he muttered. "I have to fix this once and for all."

He wouldn't tell her anymore. Honestly, she was surprised he'd told her that much. And five minutes after she left his office the speakers blared, directing Shiv Crew to Monitor One for a run.

Not Ellie's voice—he was back at her house safe and sound, busy doing shit that kept her and her household running. Her stomach tightened and a dark lump of dread took up residence in her heart when she thought about leaving him.

Leaving Ellie.

She wasn't sure she could.

But she was nearly certain she'd have to.

CHAPTER TWELVE

"You might be sick," Jack said. "He fucking left you to figure out his own shit and you might be rotting into a pile of—"

"Dammit, Jack. Shut up," she ordered.

But once again the crew was full of anger and stiff with betrayal, and she couldn't defend the berserker from it. Didn't even want to.

Only Lex stood firm in her loyalty for Strad Matheson. "He has his reasons. He loves Rune," she said, once, and then kept quiet on the subject.

Rune feared that Jack, when—if—he saw Strad again, was going to pull his gun and blow the berserker away. He was that pissed.

It had just taken a little while to sink in.

A little while for them to realize he'd really taken off.

And the entire time she argued and fought and thought and worried, she listened.

Listened for the echoes.

Terrified she'd hear them.

She and the crew had been called to a werewolf versus vampire battle in the Moor, just a mile or so from Rune's house. By the time they got there, the fight had broken up and only a small group of homeless people remained to tell the crew what had happened.

"Wolves were winning," one woman said. She grinned,

creating one deep dimple and faded blue eyes so full of mischief that Rune couldn't help but grin back.

"Any humans?" she asked.

"Twelve," the woman answered. "The vampires carried off twelve dead humans."

Rune lifted an eyebrow. "That's a lot of dead humans."

"Weren't no damn humans," another of the homeless said. A man, his face a little more lined than the woman's, his clothing a little shabbier.

He held his hands out to a trashcan fire that lit up the night and burned with crackling merriment. "And were only a couple of Others. You're a fucking liar."

Rune didn't like the way he ran his cold stare over the homeless woman's body.

"How long have you been out here?" she asked the woman.

"Just found my way to this spot tonight," she answered, and pushed her red hair back under her fuzzy knit cap. "I was in the city but…" She hesitated, then shrugged. "I had to move on."

"We got room for you here," the man said. "Long as you keep your fucking mouth shut and…" Again, his gaze roamed her body.

The woman backed away just a little, her hands clutching at the bag she held. She glanced behind her into the shadows of the night, as though looking for an escape route should she need one later.

Rune didn't like it.

Something about the woman was vaguely familiar, and it took her a few minutes to understand what it was. The homeless woman reminded Rune of her adoptive mother.

The clothes she wore, the knit cap with the faded pink flower on the front of it, even the gray sweater with the deep pockets.

And the red hair.

"Rune?" Jack asked. "You okay?"

"Yeah," she whispered.

Raze stepped forward, sensing a threat, and drew the woman's attention. "You sure are a big one, mister. What's your name?"

Raze stared over her head and said nothing.

"Do you know what the fight was about?" Denim asked her.

She gazed at him for a long, silent moment before looking at Levi. "You are a lucky woman," she told Rune. "To answer your question, pretty boy, no, I don't." She shook her head. "It was hard to figure out what they were upset about. But they dispersed almost before they assembled."

Another man at her side cleared his throat and gave the woman a look Rune was unable to decipher.

"What?" Rune asked him.

He scratched his chin and refused to meet her stare. "We don't need to be volunteering information to the law, is all."

"I'll need you to volunteer your names." She glanced around at the rest of the vagrants. "Do any of you have anything to tell us?"

"We didn't see nothing," one of them said, tossing a disgusted look at the woman who'd talked. "Nothing at all."

"Of course not," Levi said.

"I'm Jill," the talkative woman said. She nodded toward the man who stood beside her. "And I think this one's name is Lou."

Lou eyed the crew. "You ought to pay us for our information."

Rune lifted an eyebrow. "I'll send someone back with a bag of burgers, dude."

"We're not drunks," he said, and spat at her feet.

"Hey now," Jack said, giving Lou a warning shove. "You don't want to do that."

"Fuck off, you one-eyed bastard," Lou said. "And keep your fucking burgers."

"Shut up," one of the quieter men said. "We'll take them burgers."

Rune gave him a nod. "You got it."

"Rune," Owen said, glancing down at his beeping phone. "It's from the Annex. Eugene wants a meeting."

But she wasn't ready to leave. "Jill. Come with us. I'll put you up in a hotel until you get things straightened out."

"There's nothing to straighten out," Jill said, quietly. "Go mind your business, you and your team. I'll make out okay. I always do."

And in the end, Jill refused to budge and Rune had to leave. But she handed Jill a card with her phone number on it. "You need me, call me."

How awful it was to leave a woman who could have been her mother on the cold streets of River County. How hard.

But Jill wouldn't budge.

Rune stood in front of Lou for a long, long moment before finally, he looked away from the flames and into her eyes.

She dropped her fangs.

He stumbled back, away from the fire and almost into Jill. "What," he said. "What?"

Rune stepped closer to him. "You hurt her, and I will feed you your dick as you scream and beg me for mercy. I swear it." And she moved closer still. "Do you believe me?"

He nodded, fast and hard, his eyes wide. "Yeah yeah," he said, wheezing. "Yeah yeah."

She looked around at the entire group of vagrants. They'd fallen silent and watched with fear in their faces. "She's under my protection. No one touches her. You got it?"

They all nodded, then stared at the ground.

"You don't have to worry about us hurting nobody," the man who'd asked for burgers said. "We don't hurt nobody."

Rune gave Lou one last look and turned away. "What message from the Annex?" she asked, as they walked back to their cars.

"Just for all of us to see Eugene immediately," Owen answered.

Raze glared at nothing, his eyes glittering beneath the streetlights.

"What's wrong, baby? Pissed that we didn't get to fight?"

"Yeah," he said. "I am."

"Maybe Eugene will rectify that," Denim said.

"You're worried about Jill," Lex said.

"I wonder what her story is," Rune replied.

"I could have touched her," Lex said, "but some get offended when I do that."

"People like to keep their secrets," Rune said, and refrained from looking at Owen.

"And that's their right," Jack said.

She shrugged. "Yeah. Sorry, Jack."

"Sorry about what?" Levi asked.

"Quiet," Rune said, and held up a hand. "Listen."

The crew halted immediately, hands full of silver, ready.

"It's…" Lex began, then stopped and frowned.

"A fight," Rune answered.

The air was full of blood.

And she wanted it.

Suddenly, the street was teeming with Others—shifters, wolves, vampires—steaming through yards, bodies ramming houses, hitting, biting, clawing…

Fighting each other.

"Fuck me," Rune whispered.

"What the hell happened?" Jack asked. "What's happening?"

"Others against vampires," Rune said. "It's got something to do with the sickness."

"It started with the vampires," Raze said. "And the

Others are going to try to cut it off at its source."

"What do we do?" Lex asked.

Owen smiled, his gaze hot and eager beneath the battered brim of his hat. "We figure out which side we want to fight for."

"We're on the side of the humans in this fight," Rune said. "Protect the humans. The Others need to have this out." Then she grinned. "But I won't order you not to pick a side and fuck somebody up."

She dropped her fangs and shot out her claws, then ran with her crew into the fray of the battle.

She and her crew needed a fight, and it was their lucky night.

CHAPTER THIRTEEN

She'd had good intentions—to make sure no humans were caught in the middle of a vicious Other battle—but once she was in the thick of the fight, and blood was spraying, pain hitting her with comforting familiarity, rage and hunger took over.

Then all she wanted to do was release her monster and kill.

Feed, and kill.

So she did.

She didn't discriminate. If it got in her way, she was either eating it or ripping it apart.

She lost herself in the glory and the gory, as did her crew.

It was what they'd been born for. What they thrived on.

And when the battle limped to a halt, it was because dawn would soon be breaking and the vampires had to hide from the sun.

Had it not been for that, the battle, which grew larger and more violent by the hour, might have gone on until the rotting sickness wouldn't have had a chance to wipe them out. They were doing a great job of that all on their own.

Rune stood on piles of dead as the sun pointed red fingers across the sky. The bloody ground seemed reflected in the heavens, and for a long moment she had to grind her teeth and wait for the need to cry to pass.

The berserker hadn't been there. He hadn't come to help his crew, to wade into the battle with his familiar roar sounding and his deadly spear flashing.

And that hurt just a little fucking bit.

The streets were completely silent as the fighters still able surveyed the dead and began to think about the tasks ahead. They'd carry their dead and wounded home and those who had jobs would clean up and prepare for the workday.

Business as usual.

Except the panic had begun.

Rune stared out at nothing, her face and body itchy with blood and gore. She was sticky and filthy but the wounds she'd sustained by being careless were healing rapidly.

The high of the battle slunk away and left her empty and dejected.

Her mind was black.

"Rune," Lex said, standing beside her. "Don't let it take you."

Rune moved her eyes, slowly, to look at the little Other. She said nothing.

"It'll pass," Lex continued. "The…" She spread her hands, struggling to find the right words. The words that would say exactly what she meant. Finally, she just shook her head. "Don't let it take you."

But the silence had fled and Rune was dark.

"Anyone hurt?" she asked, but her voice was dull.

"Nothing major," Jack answered, watching her.

"The violence didn't help," she said suddenly.

Owen stepped forward and stood close, so close she had to crane her neck to look into his eyes. "Maybe the sex will," he murmured.

And a spark of something interested and alive flared inside her. She shivered.

The twins, surprising her, came toward her and Owen, moving as though they had the exact same thought and intention. They stopped on either side of Owen and waited until he took his gaze from Rune to look first at Levi, then Denim.

"We're not going to let you fuck her up," Levi said, his voice almost too low to hear.

"She's not herself." Denim's stare was so cold it might have frozen a lesser man into a block of solid ice. "Not yet. So you'll back off."

Rune opened her mouth, but no words came out. She was shocked, confused, and maybe just a little fucking relieved.

She realized something right then. The berserker had been her protector. And her excuse.

Not physically, really—though he had taken on that responsibility as well—but he had been there. For *her*.

Who cared as much as he did about what might happen to her?

So when he left, she felt alone.

But she was *not* alone.

She smiled and hugged the twins to her, hard, and let herself find, for them, some peace.

When she stumbled out of her own misery and fear and took a look at her people, she saw that Jack and Raze and Lex watched her with the same look the twins held.

They'd known, and they were showing her. No matter that she might decide to take on Owen, no matter what she might do. They just wanted to let her know.

Even if she didn't need anyone to protect her—she was a bad fucking monster—to them she was just Rune.

They loved her.

She glanced at Owen and he grinned at her, nothing much in his eyes but understanding. And some desire. There was that, too.

He said nothing.

"I'm going to talk to Eugene," she told them. "You all

go home and get some sleep."

"Don't be too long," Lex said, "or Ellie won't *let* us sleep."

Rune entered the Annex still covered with blood and smelling of death, but her mood had lifted and she didn't care even a little bit about the shocked looks thrown her way.

She rapped on Eugene's door, walking in when she heard him call out.

He stood up quickly when he saw her. "Jesus, Rune."

She grinned and lowered herself into a chair. "You'll have to have someone clean this chair but I don't feel like standing."

"I'll have it replaced," he said. "I'm glad you came in. I got reports, but I wanted to hear from you."

"Others were fighting the vampires. From what I could gather, the Others are pissed off and panicking because the vampires are spreading the rotting sickness."

He nodded, then gave a long, slow blink.

"Well fuck," she said. "What is it?"

"My people have been hard at work," he said. "Coffee?"

"Yeah." She waited impatiently while he called for coffee.

"Okay," he said. "If the Others didn't have the disease before the fight, they will have it now. The sickness is spread from humans to vampires through feeding. The vampires spread it to the Others through body fluids, blood…" he hesitated.

"What?"

"And air," he continued. "It's airborne."

She felt herself pale. "No."

He nodded, grim and solemn. "The Others don't have a chance. They're all going to die, and there's not one fucking thing I can do about it."

She shook her head, unable to take it in. Unable to accept it.

"The humans are carriers," he went on, "but as far as we know, they don't get sick. They pass it to the vampires through feeding—from what we know right now, the Others aren't infected by the humans. They're infected only by the vampires. So they're right to blame the vampires."

She glared at him. "No. They're not."

He spread his fingers. "I just meant the Others can't catch it from humans. The humans are carriers, vehicles. The Others catch it from the vampires in every way possible. Contact, blood, air, touch, even. The vampires are like radiation. Being near them is lethal to the Others."

"If the vampires don't feed from the humans, they'll die."

"They're going to die anyway."

"How are the humans getting the disease in the first place?"

"A few of them were likely deliberately infected, and are spreading it to each other through the usual routes—contact, body fluids, sex, even picking it up from door handles and towels. It's accelerated over the last few hours. The samples I had brought in are showing rapid decline."

"You'll have to do a press conference." She was almost unable to make her numb lips move. "Keep the humans from panicking."

She barely noticed when the coffee was brought in and handed to her. She drank half of it in one hot gulp.

"Rune." He leaned forward. "The humans will panic, no matter what I say. They're calling the sick Others *rotters*. The Others are panicking as well. River County is about to fall into chaos. Be ready."

"What can I do?"

He was silent for a long moment. "I don't know," he said, finally, and then, "I would ask that you just try to stay alive."

But he didn't sound like he had any real confidence in her ability to do so.

Part Two

THE CHAOS

CHAPTER FOURTEEN

"How is she doing?" Rune asked, staring down at the sleeping child.

Elizabeth stood stiff and silent, her hands at her sides. "She's excellent."

"But?"

Elizabeth looked at Rune, her eyes blank. "She's determined to go wherever she went when she was locked inside the net. She will only say she belongs there. I see the longing in her eyes. She wants to be there as much as I want…" She trailed off and shook her head.

Rune didn't prompt her to continue. She knew what Elizabeth had been about to say. *As much as I want her to stay.*

"I'm sorry," Rune said.

"I *love* her." Elizabeth's cool façade cracked, and sorrow oozed through the gap. "I shouldn't have allowed myself to love her."

"Of course you should. We all do." She patted Elizabeth's arm. "Fie needs all the love we can give her."

Rune understood Fie completely. She felt the call too, and it was strong enough, at times, to take her breath. Fie was a child and not equipped to understand or handle the disappointments of not getting what she so desperately needed.

Fie wanted to go. Rune did not.

Rune had talked with the child once when Elizabeth had gone to get lunch.

"Why don't you just go there, Fie, like you did when you were in the net?"

Fie's look had been one of scorn. "I don't want to leave my body here. I need all of me to go. I have to go with *you*."

"What if I can't go?"

"You can if you want to. Don't you want to?"

No. No, she didn't want to.

And Fie had known that.

Her cell rang and she answered it, glad to have a distraction from Elizabeth's misery.

"Rune," Bill Rice said, "are you close?"

"I'm in the building. What do you need?"

"Come see me."

She hung up, said goodbye to Elizabeth, and left the room. Bill had coffee waiting when she walked into his office five minutes later.

Bill nodded at the television screen on his wall, and she turned to watch after grabbing a coffee off his desk.

"Nothing new?" she asked.

"Not exactly new," he answered. "Just worse."

"Tell me."

"Fifteen human infants have been taken from hospitals, clinics, and from new parents just arriving home. Seventeen pregnant women were abducted. From Ohio. Since *Tuesday*."

She closed her eyes. They'd known it would come to that. The human unborn and newborn babies were not infected.

The vampires needed them to feed from.

And new groups of human garbage were taking and selling the infants and pregnant women to the vampires.

Not just in River County.

All over the world. It had spread that quickly.

"Last night," Bill continued, "six vampires entered the

Spiritgrove hospital and stole four newborns."

"Fuck," Rune muttered.

He nodded.

"Now," she said. "*Now* we'll have to purge the fucking bloodsuckers."

"Yes. We can't wait for the sickness to annihilate them all. Not when they're taking human children to feed from."

"They're desperate. Starving, dying, rotting—"

"Are you defending the vampires, Rune?"

She shot him a sharp glance. "Fuck you, Bill."

He sighed and rubbed his temples. "I'm sorry. It's…unimaginable. Things are changing too quickly. There's no time to try to fix it, because the world is going crazy too fast."

"Yeah. Chaos."

"Eugene is going to send you after Kelic and his children. Tonight."

She didn't say anything, just stared at the television screen with its horrific images of piles of rotted Others, dead human women, their wrists still cuffed, found in ditches after their full-term babies had been cut from their wombs.

Girls were being abducted and impregnated by human men, then sold. No matter if the girls or the seed donators were carriers of the sickness, the infants would not be.

It had been discovered that no child under one year old carried the sickness.

Infants were in high demand.

Fear and panic had taken hold of the country, and it wasn't letting go anytime soon.

"Though the Others are rotting," Rice said, "they are forming alliances to stay alive, to protect each other until…"

"There is no until." She shook her head. "Nothing will ever fix this. They will never be forgiven for what they're doing now. No matter what. You could find a cure tomorrow and the Others will still be hunted for the rest of forever."

"No," Bill disagreed. "It will only seem like forever. You know how people forget. How history repeats itself. Eventually, the Others and humans will live once again in a strange sort of harmony."

Chaos.

Chaos and doom.

The world, in a few short weeks, had completely changed.

"Still no word from Strad?" Bill asked, his voice tired.

She shook her head.

No. No word from Strad.

"He's gone to battle his personal demons, Bill. I don't know if there will ever again be any word from the berserker."

He stood and went to stand beside her. "Rune, I'd like to tell you something about love."

"Love?" she said, and snorted. But damn if she didn't have to fight to keep her bloody tears at bay.

From the corner of her eye she saw his lips move as he smiled. "Strad Matheson loves you more than I've ever seen a man love a woman. And I know a little something about love. It might not be smart, or good, or right. It just *is*."

He paused and waited until she looked at him before he continued. Maybe he wanted her to not only hear his truth, but to see it in his eyes. "Love like that will always come back, Rune. No matter where it goes or how long it stays away. Always."

"Damn you, Bill," she whispered, and dug her fingernails into her thigh. "What you're calling love is just obsession. Need. *Addiction*."

"My dear," he said, his eyebrows high. "What do you think love is?"

She couldn't reply.

He patted her shoulder with a heavy hand then went back to his desk. "Let's put love on the back burner and worry about evil."

She squared her shoulders. "Yes. And what we're going to do to defeat the son of a bitch."

"After the purge is successful, Eugene has plans to send Shiv Crew to do takedowns of known traffickers. You'll have kill orders."

"Good. Those are some kills I'll look forward to."

"When don't you?" Then he shrugged before she could retort. "He's also sending you to do purges and extract human babies and women from vampire clans all over Ohio."

"What? Leave River County?"

"After the purge."

"Shit."

"Why are you reluctant to leave the county?"

"Because we're needed here."

"You're needed everywhere, Rune. Humans are being slaughtered. Human *babies*."

"Yeah. I know. But every county has its own fucking crews. If we're not here to defend ours, you know what can happen."

"Talk to him. Tell him your concerns. He can send other crews. Not," he said, smiling slightly, "as good as your crew, but good enough to hunt vampires."

He watched her with a sharp, knowing expression.

And damned if excitement didn't uncurl in her stomach at the words *hunt vampires*.

Hunt.

She wanted to go. Wanted to go hunt the bad guys, stake vampires, get back into the routine of the good old days.

She needed to forget that she might be sucked into another world and lose her crew, her life, her*self*.

She wanted to forget that she was so fucking afraid.

She would take her crew and end the bloodsuckers.

There was no hope for them. They couldn't survive without blood, and she couldn't allow them to torture women and children to get what they needed.

Eventually, the world would create a way for the vampires to live once again with humans. In the meantime, they had to go.

Yes, they were rotting and would die anyway, but not quickly enough. Not before they killed—and turned—more humans.

Once again, the vampires were hated, hunted, and killed on sight.

Even the Annex, pro-Other, couldn't see another way out of that.

Not then.

Maybe not ever.

CHAPTER FIFTEEN

"What do you want us to do?" Lex asked. "Are we really going to purge Simon and his children today?"

"Do you know of a better way to stop them?" Rune stared moodily out of her kitchen doorway, into the mean desolation of the Moor. "We have no other choice. They've *given* us no other choice."

"I know," Lex murmured. "But it's not their fault, really. I'm devastated for them."

Me too. "We have no other choice," Rune repeated, but her voice was softer.

"There are people working on synthetic blood," Levi said. He took a cup off the countertop and poured himself some coffee.

"That might take forever," Rune said. "Labs tried making it before and it didn't sustain the vampires."

"They didn't try hard enough," Denim said. "And funding was low. No one thought it would be a money maker. Now they do."

"Maybe," Rune said. "But synthetic blood won't keep the sick vampires from rotting."

"It could keep the vampires from feeding on humans and getting infected in the first place," Denim said. "And it could stop them from abducting humans."

"They've become wild animals," Lex said. "The vampires."

The vampires hated the humans for poisoning them, and once taken, the humans did not fare well under the vampires' care.

The corpses found lying in ditches and in the woods showed chilling proof of abuse the abducted humans—children as well as adults—suffered at the hands of their captors. Whatever positive changes Simon Kelic had created in River County had evaporated almost overnight.

It began to rain, a cold drizzle that did nothing to help Rune's frame of mind. The sun was hiding, the sky was overcast and gray, and she felt every bit of it in her mood.

She and her crew would begin the hunt for Simon Kelic, and when they found him, he would die.

More vampires would come. They'd sneak into the county and go to ground, then creep out during the nights to hunt.

It was going to be a long, hard war whether she killed Simon or not.

"What if we kill him and they find a cure next week?" Lex asked. "What if?"

"We can't go on what ifs," Ellis said, his voice brusque. He bustled around the kitchen, constantly moving, not looking any of them in the eye.

He didn't want them to know how relieved he was that the humans were going to war with the vampires. Killing the vampires.

He didn't want them to know.

But they knew. Of course they knew.

Rune sighed.

"Coffee, Rune?" Ellie asked, his voice a little too high.

"No, baby. My stomach sloshes when I walk."

"Food, then. I'll cook something up. You'll need to eat before…"

"That's good, Ellie. Make us some lunch."

He was suddenly beside her, his arm around her waist. "I hate it when you're depressed. *Hate* it."

She drew back, a little, at the savagery in his tone. "I'll

be okay."

"The world is screwed, Rune. You were right. It doesn't matter what we do, does it?"

She frowned. "Ellie?"

"Ellis," Levi said. "Don't."

"You're dying this time," Ellis said, ignoring Levi. "We all know it. It'll take longer to destroy you than normal Others, but you're dying. Maybe your brain will remain, and we'll scoop it up out of the goo and plop it into a glass so we can—"

"Ellis," Lex screamed. "Shut your motherfucking *mouth*."

Ellis shuddered, then covered his face and started sobbing.

"Fuck me," Rune said, and went back to staring out into the cold.

"Dammit, Levi," Denim muttered. "Help him."

Because Rune couldn't.

Owen took Ellis by the shoulders and walked him to Levi, then went back to stand beside her. "You need to find your guts," he said, quietly. "Let your anger out or your fear is going to control you."

He was right. She *wasn't* angry—at least not angry enough. She was afraid, yes. But what held her in a soul-crushing grip wasn't the fear, it was the bleakness. The desolation.

The uncertainty.

"I need to reboot," she murmured. And she had no idea how to do that.

"Get out of your own head," he said. "That's how you do it."

She looked at him. He stood slumped against the doorframe, as unaffected by the cold as she was. His hair streamed over his shoulders, and his face was emotionless. Gun belts, holstered weapons, and silver blades decorated his lean body.

"Owen," she said.

"Yes?"

"Who *are* you?"

He took a drink of his coffee. "I'm your friend, Rune."

She smiled. "Yeah."

He straightened and placed his cup on the table. "Come with me."

"Where are we going?"

"We're going to hunt for some traffickers to kill. I just got a lead. Then we're going to find and purge the vampires while they're still asleep. No sense in wasting any more time."

Eugene had assigned other teams to the normal happenings of the county. Shiv Crew was to search out and destroy all vampires.

That was all. And that was everything.

She put it off. She didn't really want to go after Simon.

But she'd decided to wait for night because that's when the assholes would come out to feed. It'd be easier than the almost impossible task of finding the underground nests into which they'd gone to sleep.

She nodded and gave him a lingering look. "Okay. Ellie, forget the food. Call Jack and Raze for me. They'll be here by the time I weapon up, and we'll get started." She strode from the kitchen, throwing back over her shoulder, "Wear your vests."

She heard Owen begin to bark commands as she left the room.

"Levi, make sure the kill kits are stocked in the cars. Ellis, pack some sandwiches and a couple thermoses of coffee. Denim…"

His voice faded away as she made her way to her bedroom, but the feeling of hope in her chest grew stronger.

They'd been through bad shit too many times to count. For them, it was a way of life. It was even a comfort.

The hesitation and doubt were what killed her spirit.

Kill vampires? Rot into a useless puddle?

Lose the *berserker?*

She let it go. What came would come, and she was going to do her best to kick its ass when it got there.

She found her guts.

CHAPTER SIXTEEN

"If it's hostile or sick," she said, "kill it."

The corners of the cowboy's eyes crinkled as he grinned down at her. "Welcome back."

"Thanks for helping me out of the black," she replied, but she didn't return his smile.

"I didn't do anything."

"You reminded me. Now shut the fuck up. We don't have time for a powwow."

He nodded, but his smile lingered. "I'll protect every part of you, Rune. I'll always have your back." Then he shrugged. "For as long as it's possible."

"That comes with being on this team," Levi said. "We'll all protect her."

"And each other," Lex added.

"Hugs and kisses and goddamn happy faces," Jack growled. "Can we just get a move on?" He yanked a silver blade the size of his forearm from its sheath. "Those heads aren't going to decapitate themselves."

Raze almost smiled. "Let's move."

Soon it would be dark. They'd already slain so many hostiles they were wearing blood like a layer of skin, and they hadn't even made it into Wormwood.

The cemetery was full of sick Others, and word had reached her that traffickers were also hiding inside the magical gates.

And the vampires would be rising.

Dying.

Now that she'd made up her mind, had hardened her heart to what she had to do, she was eager to get it done.

Simon would know she was coming, and he would know she had no choice.

He'd been sending his children after the 'pure' humans—infants. And he'd been slaughtering pregnant women. He was buying from traffickers.

They all were.

Yeah. He knew she was coming.

He wouldn't know that she'd find him, though.

Or maybe he was too sick to care.

Ellie had tried to convince Levi to wear his fang necklace. Levi had just snorted and refused to entertain the notion, and eventually Ellis had dropped the vampire repellent back under his shirt.

She had some moments of bittersweet nostalgia as she led her crew, blades and vguns ready, through Wormwood.

Suddenly Raze, as they loped through the graveyard, pulled a small silver axe and sent it whirling through the air. It buried itself in the back of a wolf's head.

No warning, no hesitation.

"Raze," Rune said, stopping at the side of the dead wolf. "He doesn't look sick and he didn't approach us. Why'd you kill him?"

"If it's Other, it's dying," Raze said, yanking free his axe. "He would soon be sick, if he wasn't yet."

Lex made a sound, drawing their gazes.

She looked toward Raze, her eyes jerking, horrified. "What's *wrong* with you?"

He closed his eyes for a long second, drawing in a deep breath. "I'm sorry."

"Rune and I are Others," she said, furious. "Will you kill us as well?" She strode to him, then bared her neck. "Go on. Cut off my head."

"Lex," he started, and reached out to touch her

shoulder.

She jerked away from him. "Fuck you, asshole."

"Lex," Levi said. "Calm down. We have orders. The Others are spreading the rotting sickness. They're killing humans. We have no choice."

"It's them or us," Denim agreed.

"*I'm* a them," she said.

Raze looked at Rune. "What are we doing?"

She repeated her earlier words. "If it's hostile or sick, kill it."

"Kind of hard to figure that out from a distance," Jack said.

Lex put her hands to her head. "It's so confusing."

"I know," Rune answered. It *was* confusing. Did they kill indiscriminately? Or did they give those few Others who weren't sick a chance?

"Rune?" Levi asked.

"Okay, here's the deal. Kill if you know the Other is sick or hostile. If you don't know and aren't attacked, leave it alone. Good enough?"

Because in the end, the Others were going to be wiped out anyway. Lex could have her moment to think otherwise if she needed it.

Jack nodded. "Okay then."

"Gunnar," Owen said.

The ghoul had been standing in the shadows of the trees long enough to know exactly what they were discussing. "Do not attack," he called. "I would speak with you, Your Slaughterousness."

"I'll be right back," she told her crew, and jogged to him.

"You have fed?" he asked, when she stood in front of him.

She frowned. "Not for a while." *Not since the fucking berserker.*

"It is good that you have your crew to keep you alive. They will feed you."

"Yeah. What's up, sexy?"

"Will you slay me if I take the sickness?" he asked, his dark eyes worried.

"You're not killing humans, are you?"

He put his nose into the air. "Most certainly not."

"Then I'm not killing you." She paused, studying his worn face carefully. "You okay?"

"You mustn't worry about me—we shall worry about you. It is my hope that with the magic inside you, you will defeat any harm that may come to you."

She put a hand to her chest. "There's a chance I won't get sick?"

He widened his eyes. "Rune, there is always hope. That is what I want you to remember. There is always hope. No matter how dire things may seem."

She let the hope sink in. She might not get sick. She might not.

"What do you know, Gunnar? You're warning me about something specific."

"You're going to see Damascus. You are in need of a warning."

She shook her head. "No. If she doesn't somehow suck me in, I'm not going anywhere. If she makes it here again, I'll run to meet the bitch and do everything I can to slaughter her. But I'm not leaving."

He let her talk, patient, quietly watching her.

It was not reassuring. "I'm *not* going there, Gunnar."

"Your Highness," he said, gently. "You will go."

She shuddered. "Fuck," she whispered. "When?"

He shrugged. "How would *I* know?"

"Damn you, ghoul. What do you want?"

He still wasn't back to his old self. His hair was stringier than usual, his eyes were more sunken, and he was skinnier. Everything he was, only exaggerated.

He pushed his hair out of his face. "There is a cure for the rotting sickness, Your Highness."

She opened her mouth, but only a squeak escaped.

He waited patiently for her to find her voice.

"A cure? A fucking cure?" She grabbed the front of his tattered shirt to drag him to her, and Dawn slunk from the darkness of the thick trees, her fingers curled into talons.

Rune didn't care about the female ghoul. "*Where*, Gunnar? Where is the cure?"

"Take your hands off him," Dawn said. "Or you won't have a chance to find out."

Gunnar waved her away. "Rune. You know where the cure is."

"The Next didn't create this infection?"

"No human group is that powerful or full of magic." He bowed his head. "I am sorry."

She let go of him. "Fuck me."

He nodded. "This is why you will go there, Your Horror."

But she shook her head. "No."

"It is fearsome, that world," he said. "But you will not falter. It is what you must do."

"I can't, Gunnar."

"You will come back."

"I *can't*."

"You will come back."

"But what if I don't?"

He was quiet for a long moment, his black eyes studying her with too much knowledge. "If you don't, then this world will fall into chaos and all Others will die—and you will live forever in the world of Damascus."

She said nothing. Nothing, until Dawn slipped up beside her, leaned down to peer into her face, and whispered, "Your demon is sick."

It took a full minute for Rune to understand what she meant, and when she finally did, she stumbled back, crying out in disbelief.

The crew came to her then. Including Lex.

"What happened?" Raze asked.

Rune could barely make her body work. In slow

motion, she turned her head to look at Lex.
"No," Raze said. "Don't say that, Rune."
Lex began shivering. "I…oh," she said.
Lex had been exposed. She was sick.
Oh, God.
She was sick.

CHAPTER SEVENTEEN

They went to work that evening with desperation, horror, and fury. The Others of Wormwood watched the crew coming, and from shadows and sickness, they went to meet them.

Wormwood seemed to watch them all with contempt and its own share of ferocious wrath. The trees awakened, seizing people and Others alike, lifting roots to trip them, snaking out impenetrable vines to snag ankles and necks.

Wormwood came alive, and it was angry.

Sounds of battles spread throughout the vast graveyard. Blood sprayed and hung heavy in the air along with the screams and cries of injured and desperate fighters. The cold ground became muddy and messy with gallons of blood and steaming hot organs.

"Do not split up," Rune yelled to her crew, once, when they were nearly overwhelmed by the sheer numbers of sick and terrified Others.

Occupied as they were, purging the vampires was the last thing on their minds—until the vampires decided to play.

The day had fled beneath the onslaught of violence and night came eagerly, waking the bloodsuckers.

The starving, sick bloodsuckers.

The moon sagged with grief, looming large and pale above the horror of the killing ground.

"I can't bring my demon," Lex screamed, but she fought alongside Rune as she had before her demon had clawed its way into existence.

Mirrored, mimicked, and killed.

And grew sicker by the second, at least it seemed so to Rune's worried mind.

Rune wasn't rotting.

Lex was rotting.

Dozens of Others fell beneath the blades of the crew, but some simply curled up and died. Some of the very sick ones still tried to fight, and Rune got an up-close and personal look at what it would be like to get the sickness.

She went after one of them with her claws inches away from taking his head, when she stopped and drew back, fighting not to cover Lex's sightless eyes.

The sick shifter put his hands to his face. His features melted and ran between his fingers. He fell to the ground, trying to shift, but was unsuccessful.

When they got to a certain point, they couldn't shift.

"I can't bring my demon…"

Too bad most of the Others weren't yet to that point—they shifted and fought the way no human could fight.

Except for Shiv Crew.

Rune lost herself in the battle, in the fight to help her people stay alive. In killing the Others.

It was a losing battle.

There were simply too many of them. She realized nearly every Other in the county had fled to Wormwood. They'd thought to find a haven there, perhaps, and the graveyard, huge as it was, easily contained them all.

Wormwood was their territory, and they were determined to defend themselves against law enforcement, humans, and Rune.

Lex screamed suddenly, and Rune glanced away from a bloody vampire to find the girl on her knees, a shaggy werewolf at her back.

She was throwing up, too sick to continue fighting.

Before Rune could help her, Raze was there, driving a blade through the were's neck and plucking Lex from the ground.

He looked at Rune and waited for her sharp nod before he trotted away, carrying Lex to safety.

Leaving the rest of the crew to fight without him.

He'd be back when he could get back.

From the corner of her eye she saw a werewolf attack a shifter who'd pissed him off—and then it was a matter of seconds before the Others were fighting each other.

Unintentionally helping the crew.

She fought like a killing machine—cold and capable and so very deadly—as the worries about everything else dimmed to a faded whisper on the edge of her mind.

She killed her own, the vampires she'd been sent to purge, and the Others who clung to their lives with a senseless desperation.

But right then she wasn't Other, she wasn't vampire, and she wasn't human.

She was simply the monster.

And she was nearly unstoppable.

Her crew though, they were not.

Levi danced backward, blade in one hand and gun in the other, and tripped over a half-shifted Other who'd crawled through the cold, bloody mud, leaving body parts behind as he moved.

When Levi stumbled and fell, he was done. It was a hesitation he couldn't afford, and every Other close enough to see and unoccupied enough to take him closed in.

When Levi fell, Denim, as though tied to his twin by an invisible rope, fell with him. He was back up in a millisecond, hacking and slicing through the Others who were trying to kill his brother.

But there were simply too fucking many of the sons of bitches.

Rune ran to help, her speed rivaled only by her

strength, and ran her claws through every enemy body between her and the twins.

Jack bellowed, and she recognized his injured tone—pain and indignation in equal parts—and for the first time that night it really hit her that they might lose. That she might lose her crew.

She screamed.

And a voice answered, a voice so filled with rage there was no other word for it but death. Death answered her.

Gooseflesh covered her skin, and she trembled even as she ran, as the roar came again, closer, closer...

Owen fought free of the Others surrounding him and sprinted to her side, helping her cut through the tangled mass of Others who had the twins cornered.

"What the fuck," he yelled, his voice strained and panting, "was *that?*"

"That was rage," she answered. "And it's coming to help."

At last.

She saw him then, in the moonlight, surrounded by shadows misty with droplets of blood, coming for her.

To her.

Others fell beneath his rage and his spear—those who didn't fall ran—and she had a moment to realize they were more afraid of him, perhaps, than they were of her.

Berserker.

She felt the sting of Other claws slicing through her shoulder, her neck, her stomach, because she'd been distracted by her berserker.

But it didn't matter.

She'd survive.

"Berserker," she screamed. *"Berserker!"*

He was shirtless, weaponless but for his spear, his big body crisscrossed with wounds and bruises and blood, and she knew they were from more than the Others he was fighting then.

Something had happened to Strad Matheson.

And finally, he reached her.

There was no time to talk, but he looked at her.

Once, before he battered away the Others who dared attack what was his—his woman, his crew—

In his eyes was the truth.

They were *his*.

And he would never have left them.

Not if he'd had the choice.

It took her breath, that look.

Just a second, a moment, a slow motion lifetime of truth.

"I'll never leave you, Rune."

And he wouldn't.

She turned away, fighting with an intensity tempered by the words running through her mind…

He hadn't left.

He'd been taken.

CHAPTER EIGHTEEN

And near dawn, the vampires fled. The Others who still lived followed.

The crew stood over the dead and dying, staring at each other, unable, for a few minutes, to speak.

They let blood drip from their blades as they acknowledged their wounds and allowed a tiredness that went beyond exhaustion to overtake them.

The fight was over.

And they lived on.

Good job, sweet thing.

She smiled.

"Berserker," she murmured, and they all turned to look at the black-haired giant who stood with them.

"You thought I left you," he said.

She said nothing and found it difficult to look into his eyes.

He strode to her then, snatched her off the ground and into his arms. He held her with so much force a human would have been crushed.

But *he* was crushed. He was crushed, and she deserved to take a little of the pain.

"Don't ever give up on me," he said. "Not even when I make you think you should."

"You were gone," she replied, her voice tight, her throat hurting.

He closed his eyes for a long, tortured second. "I know. I told you I'd never leave you." His voice was deep and dark and it pierced her mind with the pain it held. "But I did."

The dam burst then, and the emotions she'd held in check fought free, exploding from her damaged heart.

"Strad," she whispered, and wrapped her arms around his neck. She buried her face against his warm, familiar flesh. He was alive, he was there, and he hadn't left.

"What happened?" Jack asked, unwilling to give them more than a couple of minutes. "How the fuck did *you* get taken?" His voice was still suspicious, still unsure.

Strad ignored him and his anger. "Where's Lex?" Lex, the only one who'd believed in the berserker's loyalty.

Rune squeezed his neck. "Put me down." And once her feet touched the ground, she turned to Raze. "Where did you take her?" she asked.

"To the cars."

"How badly was she injured?" Strad asked, his eyes narrowing.

"She wasn't injured," Rune said. But she couldn't say the words.

"She's sick," Denim said. "She's…" Then he widened his eyes and looked at Levi. "Levi. She's *sick*."

Levi shook his head in silent denial.

Raze growled and waved his bloody hands impatiently. "She's special. Nothing is happening to her."

There was no doubt in his mind. If there had been, he'd have crumbled.

The rest of them weren't so confident.

Owen walked away, his hand to his ribs. None of them called him back.

But he looked at her once, just once before he left, and his glance was bright with resolve.

She lingered on his retreating figure, but only for a moment. "Everyone to the Annex to get patched up. We need to get Lex checked out as well." She took the berserker's hand. "And while we're there, you can tell us what the fuck happened to you."

He nodded, so covered with blood she couldn't tell how injured he was. Just like the rest of them.

She knew her hungry stare was eating his face, *devouring* it, and she didn't really care who saw her need. "I am so fucking glad you're…"

Alive, here, back.

Mine.

He grinned and squeezed her hand.

They walked from the graveyard more gingerly than when they'd walked in, a line of tired, injured warriors.

But the despair was less.

At least for her.

Fuck me.

"I got a text," Strad said, later.

They'd had their wounds stitched and tended and had been debriefed—all of them but Owen. She hadn't seen him since he'd left them at Wormwood.

They'd had their showers, had downed countless pots of coffee and sandwiches, and were waiting for word from Annex doctors about Lex's illness.

Maybe it was something else. Maybe it wasn't the rotting sickness.

Maybe.

Eugene had ensconced her into the Annex clinic, promising them that his people were hard at work on an antidote.

He seemed optimistic.

Rune didn't believe his assurances for a second, but understood he needed to keep the crew somewhat hopeful.

Especially the twins.

The conference room in which they sat was warm and dim, and Rune had been dozing in her chair when the berserker's voice roused her.

"Who texted you?" Levi asked. He stood against the

wall with Denim. Whether they meant to or not, the twins closed ranks when one of them or Lex was in serious trouble.

"I have—*had*—a connection named Suzanne. She told me she'd found a link to…"

"Go on," Rune said, her voice steady. "To what?"

"To the baby," he said. "To the black-haired baby I promised to find for you."

She put her fist to her stomach. "The baby? You got a lead on the baby?"

His long hair, still damp from his shower, slid over his shoulders when he shook his head. "It was a lie. There were no leads. And Suzanne is dead." He met her stare, his own emotionless and dark. "It was a trap."

She frowned, but said nothing, just waited for him to continue.

"How the fuck," Jack asked, again, "did you get taken?"

"I was careless," Strad answered, calmly.

Rune knew exactly how he'd walked into a trap. His mind had been on her. On fulfilling a promise to her. On imagining her joy when he brought her a fat, healthy, black-haired newborn. So he'd been careless.

She stood, not looking away from him, and walked to where he sat. Without hesitating, she leaned over, wrapped her arms around his neck, and kissed him.

She closed her eyes and let her kiss say everything she wanted to say but couldn't.

The conference room faded away. There was nothing but the berserker opening his mouth against hers, nothing but his tongue, nothing but his warm, sweet breath.

He buried his fingers in her hair and held her to him, and had she wanted to pull away, he wouldn't have allowed it.

And finally, when he let her go, the room was empty.

Except for Owen.

She'd been so wrapped up in Strad she hadn't heard him come into the room. Hadn't even heard the others leaving.

He leaned back in his chair, watching them, his eyes…

God, what is that in his eyes?

Despair?

She couldn't tell. Couldn't read him.

The berserker pushed her gently away and stood. He padded to Owen, who tilted his head back to look up at the other man.

"Fuck you," Owen said.

Strad smiled, but it wasn't even close to being a real smile. *"Now,"* he said, "She's mine. You'll leave her alone." He lowered his voice. "This time I'll kill you. You won't get another warning."

His voice was almost casual.

Owen took his time standing, but when he was on his feet he got into the berserker's space. "Your warnings don't matter to me. *She* does."

Both men touched their blades, their bodies humming with energy. They stared at each other, silent.

Rune walked away, her steps not quiet, but neither man called her back.

So she left them to their shit and went to see Lex.

CHAPTER NINETEEN

"Who would want to take Strad Matheson," Bill asked. "And why didn't they kill him?"

She shook her head and stared through the glass window at Lex, glad of Bill's company. "No idea. He doesn't know, either."

Lex moved restlessly, then sat up and turned her face toward the window, as though she knew Rune and Bill were there, watching her.

Doubtlessly she did.

"They just held him," Bill said. "Didn't ask him any questions, didn't try to sell him to us, didn't explain why they wanted him."

"They beat the fuck out of him," Rune said. "They did that."

Whoever they were.

"I imagine," Bill said, his voice slightly dry, "that he wasn't exactly a quiet, obedient prisoner."

She smiled. "Nope."

Then she sobered. His wrists had been cut nearly to the bone from his attempts to free himself. The bastards who'd held him had beaten him with clubs to calm him down.

It hadn't worked.

In the end, he'd been freed—by Gunnar and Dawn.

Two of his guards had stayed with him after the other

two had left.

"Gunnar didn't have a chance to kill either guard," the berserker had said. *"The female with him took care of them in seconds and without hesitation. And she had a good time doing it."*

She'd talk to Gunnar as soon as she had a chance. He would know something about the berserker's abductors. She hoped.

"I told you I knew a little something about love," Bill said.

She lifted an eyebrow. "While you're in a gabby mood, Bill, why don't you tell me what's going on with you?" She waited until he looked at her. "Who is fucking with you? You know I'd take care of it."

He stuck his hands in his trouser pockets. "I can handle my own problems. But thank you. If there's a time when I need you to step in, I'll be sure to notify you."

She held up her hands. "Fine. I just want you to know I'm here."

"I always know that."

They watched Lex for five minutes before either of them spoke again.

"She isn't going to get better, is she?"

He was silent for a moment. "No."

"I don't know what to do, Bill. We can't lose her. There has to be something we can do."

"Eugene is working on it."

"She can't call her demon. I tried feeding her. Didn't help."

"Even your blood and bite can't fix this. Eugene told me…"

"What?" Were they keeping shit from her? Yeah. And she wasn't surprised.

"He said he's never seen anything like this."

She blew out a hard breath. "Because it's not from here."

He nodded.

"I have to go there," she said. "I have to find the cure.

Bring it back—"

"Save the world," he said. "You have to save the world."

"I have to save Lex," she murmured. "The world be damned."

One of hers was the only thing strong enough to send her to Damascus. A world full of rotting Others wouldn't have motivated her to go.

She didn't care if that was selfish.

Because every time she thought about going to the other world, something stirred inside her.

Gave her a bad, bad feeling.

Going there was not a good idea. But she would go.

"Will you tell Lex you're going?" Bill asked.

"Yeah. But I'm sure she already knows."

And if the rotting sickness didn't kill Lex first, the withdrawals would. So Rune had to hurry. She *couldn't* get trapped there.

Couldn't.

"The crew?"

"I don't know. I don't even know how I'll get there. Or when. Or if the crew can cross over with me. I just…" She punched her thigh. "I don't fucking *know.*"

And she was alone.

"If you can take them, you should take them." He looked at her then, and as she had a long time ago, she got a sudden sense that she knew nothing about him. Not really.

"Too risky."

"They belong to you."

"Yeah," she said. "I can't save the world all by myself." She tried a grin, but was pretty sure she failed.

"You probably could," he said, mildly, "but you shouldn't have to."

Suddenly uncomfortable, she changed the subject. "How's Fie?"

Only that wasn't really changing the subject. Both of

them knew Fie wanted to go with her. Maybe *needed* to go with her.

The mystery that was Fie…

"George is dead," Bill said, suddenly.

"Fuck no," she said. "Why wasn't I told?"

"You were busy."

"What happened?"

"He just stopped breathing." He hesitated. "The same night Fie broke free of her net."

She looked at him.

"Coincidence," he said.

"Elizabeth—"

"Didn't want you to know," he interrupted.

"Why the fuck not?"

He said nothing.

"The world's an asshole," she said. And Elizabeth didn't want her blaming Fie.

"Yes" he agreed. "And it's spewing shit all over us."

She was flying blind. Much more blind than Lex.

She knew nothing at all.

Nothing.

And maybe, no one.

CHAPTER TWENTY

She parked outside her house, trying to pretend her heart wasn't racing at the thought of lying once again in the berserker's arms.

Nothing was right with the world, not really—but there was that one little thing that gave her some peace.

Lying with the berserker.

Thoughts of fucking Owen didn't disappear just because Strad Matheson existed. They were still there, still strong, and still made her shiver with anticipation.

But the berserker…

Would she eventually taste Owen, try him out, give in to her desire to see what he'd be like naked and hot and rough?

Owen called to her, no matter how hard Strad might wish otherwise.

Someday she might answer.

Maybe.

"But today is not that day," she murmured.

So she strode toward her house, her mind eager with thoughts of the waiting berserker and dark with thoughts of the cowboy.

When Owen stepped out of the shadows at the corner of her house, she wasn't surprised even a little bit.

"One thing," he said, before she could speak.

"What?"

He smiled slightly and walked to her, and when he was standing close enough to touch her, he pushed back his hat and stared down at her with unreadable eyes.

"Owen. You shouldn't." She sounded weak.

Where the cowboy was concerned, she was so fucking weak.

"You and I aren't finished, Rune. No matter what happens, just remember that. We're not finished."

"What's going to happen?" she asked, frowning.

"Just…" He shook his head, then leaned down until his lips almost touched hers. "When you're fucking him, remember how it feels to want me."

He grabbed her hand and pressed it against the front of his jeans.

She shuddered. "God, Owen. Fuck." And before she pulled away, she squeezed the hard bulge straining beneath the soft fabric of his clothes.

She wanted him. That wasn't even a question.

That didn't make her a bad person. It made her…human.

She took a deep breath and stepped back. "Go home, cowboy."

He slid his hot, hot stare to her lips. "My time will come."

"You need to stay out of the berserker's way." She stepped past him, then turned back. "You're part of Shiv Crew. I don't want to lose you." Then, she went on, almost unwilling to let the next words leave her mouth. "You need to stop chasing me. I have to get shit straight in my head. You got it?"

Yeah, maybe it was more than that, but that was all she was willing to say.

He refused to answer, just watched her, his eyes narrowed and glittering with need. Desire.

She felt his hot stare on her back all the way to the house. Even after she slipped inside and shut the door behind her, after she leaned against it trying to get her breath back, she felt his stare.

Fucking cowboy.

"Rune."

"Fuck!" She put a hand to her chest. "Dammit, Berserker."

He leaned against the wall, his big arms crossed, watching her.

Shit.

"I'm going to have to kill him."

"No, you're not." She hoped her hand wasn't shaking when she pushed her hair out of her eyes. "I belong to no one but my fucking monster."

"You're wrong," he said, and like a snake, he uncoiled and shot a hand out to grab her wrist.

She jerked free, but even as strong as she was it took some effort.

She walked past him, down the hall and into her bedroom, his presence behind her making the fine hair rise on the back of her neck.

As though he were a threat.

The kind of threat she liked.

Fuck me.

She shuddered.

She wasn't ready for him when he turned her toward him and forced her wrists behind her back. He held her tightly, painfully, with one hand, tangling his other hand in her hair. "You need the danger of him," he said.

The berserker used to scare you…

She started to speak, to deny, maybe, but all that came out was a ragged breath.

"Do you trust me?" he asked.

She just stared at him, unable to say a word.

"Trust me, Rune," he murmured.

"I'm fucked up," she whispered, not even sure if she'd spoken the words or thought them.

"I love you. But I can't be everything you need me to be until you trust me." He tightened his grip on her wrists.

"Until you believe that I fucking love you."

Still, she said nothing, just stared up into his eyes.

"I see the anger in your face," he said, his voice soft, and so dark. "But I don't give a fuck for your anger. I know it's the only defense you have."

He massaged the back of her head, gently. "I need only one thing from you. Your trust. When you trust me, you'll know I'll never hurt you again on purpose. When you trust me, you'll understand that no matter what you do, no matter what you say or where you go or who you fuck, I'm not going anywhere."

Bloody tears begin to itch their way down her cheeks before he was even close to being finished speaking.

"But if I want to kill a motherfucker for touching you, I'll kill him. That's not up to you. Do you understand?"

Yeah, she understood.

She didn't control the berserker.

"I miss Z," she said, before she even knew she needed to say it. "I miss him so fucking much."

He sighed and released her wrists, then wrapped her in his arms. "I know."

He didn't ask her what Z had to do with anything.

There was no need. He already knew.

Owen is not Z.

But if Owen weren't careful, he'd be dead.

Just like Z.

CHAPTER TWENTY-ONE

She fed.

And she fed the berserker.

When she slept in the warm hardness of his arms, she slept like the dead. Nothing bothered her. Her sleep was dreamless. There were no haunting voices, no accusing eyes, no rotting friends.

But Eugene didn't allow her peace for long. Before the night was half over, he called her and the crew in. Kelic's vampires, the ones she had been unable to purge the first time out, were in Spiritgrove.

They weren't even trying to hide. Simon himself had broken into the hospital and carried out a woman who, even as he spirited her from the building, was in the middle of giving birth.

Simon was not yet sick.

Why some of them remained healthy while some of them rotted within days was a mystery—but the witnesses at the hospital assured her that Simon was not sick.

And those who were sick decided that by feeding on the pure, they'd lose their rot—or at least stay alive until a cure was found for them.

Even if the pure was an infant.

She understood Kelic. Understood his desperation. She didn't want to kill him…

But she would.

She just had to find the son of a bitch. The first purge had been unsuccessful. The second one couldn't be.

"Levi," she said, before they left the house. It would just take a few minutes to feed the twins, and though they wouldn't ask, she could see the need in their eyes.

He and Denim offered her their wrists obediently. She bit Levi, then Denim, under the somewhat narrow gaze of the berserker.

And once at the Annex, she took ten minutes to stand at Lex's bedside so the little Other could feed from her energy before she met her crew in the lobby.

"We'll split up," she told them. "Berserker, you take Denim. Levi, go with Raze. Jack, Owen. I'll go alone." She left the Annex with them, determined that before any of them went home again, the vampires of River County would be finished.

They had two hours before dawn—but it didn't matter to the crew if the vampires were awake and ready to fight or asleep and helpless. It couldn't.

"You take Denim," Strad said, as they walked across the parking lot. "I don't need backup."

The twins were as full of energy from the feeding as she was, and Denim waited impatiently to see whose car he'd be getting into.

"And I do?" Rune asked. "Don't fight me on this. Denim's with you. I'm not taking a car."

"Let's do this," Levi said, his lean body humming with eagerness.

Rune grinned. "Go kick ass, my bloodthirsty crew." Then she lost her smile and stared at them somberly. "If you see the bloodsuckers, call us in. Don't take them on until we get there. And don't any of you die on me."

As though her order would make them live.

Owen stuck his hands in his pockets. "Don't worry so much." He looked at Strad. "No one is dying."

Strad caught Owen's stare and they glared at each other for thirty seconds before Rune snapped them out of it.

"Fuck both of you. Stop your shit and be my fucking team."

But she worried about them the entire time she roamed River County, trying to sniff out the vampires.

The first place she searched was Wormwood. She didn't really expect the vampires to hide in the cemetery—there were too many Others there who'd be willing to turn them in.

But she had to check.

Gunnar was waiting for her. "There are no vampires here."

"I didn't really think there would be." She looked around. "It's empty here. Quiet."

"The Others are dying quickly." He stared at her.

"I'll go when I can go, Gunnar. I haven't heard any echoes."

"Then you're not listening hard enough," Dawn said, stepping from the shadows. "If you really want to go, you'll go."

"I wish it were that easy," Rune said. "But from where I stand it's almost fucking impossible."

Dawn rolled her eyes. "You're scared."

Rune lifted her eyebrow at Dawn's disdain. "Yeah? Are you going to tell me Damascus doesn't scare you?" She frowned. "Who the hell are you, anyway?"

"That," Gunnar said hurriedly, "is a long story. Go to the clinic in Willowburg, Your Horror. They will direct you to some of the vampires."

"The clinic? Are they—"

"Go," he said. "Time is running out. For all of us."

She stared at him a moment longer. "You're not sick, are you?"

Dawn answered for him. "He is rotting, Your Dumbness. If you don't go to Skyll, he will die with the others."

Rune put a hand to her chest. "Fuck, Gunnar." Then, "Skyll? That's what her world is called?"

"Skyll is the rim of horror," Gunnar said. "Limbus. Limbo. The border between. And I will be fine."

"Yes," Dawn agreed. "If Her Creepiness doesn't hide in a corner sobbing in fear."

"Listen, ghoul. Gunnar can call me whatever he wants to call me. You can't. Keep your fucking mouth shut or when I do go, I'm hauling your ass back there with me."

Dawn paled and took a step back. "You…"

"Yes?"

"Go away."

Rune went. If Dr. Haas, the Other doctor, could tell her where the vampires were, she had no time to waste.

She called Jack once she was outside Wormwood. "Pick me up at the cemetery. We need to go to the clinic in Willowburg. Gunnar says they'll have a lead on some of the vampires."

"You got it," he said. "Want me to call the others?"

"Yeah." It wasn't quite daylight and the vampires were still awake. The entire crew would need to be there. The vampires might be sick but they were able to fight.

And run.

She didn't know why she'd called Jack to pick her up instead of Strad or Raze. He pulled up and Owen jumped out, giving her a wink before he got into the backseat.

She'd forgotten Owen was with Jack or she might have called someone else. But then she brushed the thought away. She wasn't walking on eggshells because of Owen *or* the berserker.

Once she was inside the car she punched in the clinic number. She'd let them know she was on her way to see the doctor.

No one answered.

"Shit."

"What is it?" Jack asked.

"Drive faster, baby. There's no answer at the clinic."

She caught glimpses of sick Others, some lying dead at the sides of the highways, others walking aimlessly as decaying bodies and splintering minds overtook them.

As they drew closer to Willowburg they spotted a group of Others gathered in a field off the road—they would never have seen them if the headlights hadn't, for one brief second, glanced off the lifeless body of a human hanging over a low hanging branch of a tree.

"It's not a group of Others," Rune told Jack and Owen. "It's a mob of vampires. Don't get careless."

Jack slammed on the brakes and all three of them were out of the car in seconds. Rune smelled the sickness as soon as she left the vehicle.

Some of the vampires were sick, some of them were not. Two healthy bloodsuckers ran to meet the crew, equal parts determination and madness in their pale faces.

Three more followed, blood leaking from stained lips.

A female vampire stood, then listed to the side and lay without moving.

Rune processed it all in seconds, then there was little time for anything but killing.

"Human," she heard Owen shout, and caught a glimpse of him pulling an unmoving woman from the ground.

He tossed her over his shoulder, wielding his blade with one hand as he backed away from the group of vampires.

The vampires weren't overly interested in the woman Owen carried, which told Rune they'd already gotten everything they could from her. She was either already dead or would be dead in a matter of minutes.

She didn't see Simon or Iker. Likely the master had been trying to keep some sort of peace and the band she was facing were rogues who'd split from him.

And they were angry.

A bloodsucker ran at her, his fangs flashing. Before he could reach her, another vampire appeared, shoved him away, and went for Rune himself. Snarling, raging, hungry.

Sick.

They blamed her for the sickness as much as they blamed the humans. Blamed her for not saving them. And they all wanted a piece of her.

She understood.

That didn't mean she wouldn't have to kill them.

And the sun was coming.

The vampires were so fucked up they didn't seem to see or feel or *hear* dawn breaking—and as Rune readied her claws to dig out her attacker's heart, the sun did it for her.

Just that suddenly, the bloodsuckers began screaming as they melted and burned in a hideous show of agony, crying out in terror as the reaper came to tote them off after centuries of life.

Rune covered her ears and closed her eyes, unable to bear witness to a kind of suffering that not even she had been forced to endure.

When she was able to look again, the sun was smiling, and the vampires were dead.

CHAPTER TWENTY-TWO

"You okay?" Jack asked, adjusting his eye patch.

Owen stood silently at the car, staring off into the distance. The woman he'd carried away had died before he'd gotten her out of the field.

The vampires had ripped her baby from her before she'd died. When Rune forced herself to search the field she'd found the body of the infant. She'd placed it with its mother in the back of Jack's car.

Then she stood still, numb, cold, and so very tired.

"Rune," Jack said, gently. "We need to go to the clinic. That wasn't all of them."

She nodded. "No sign of Simon or Iker?"

"No."

Maybe Iker had died early. Maybe Simon had killed him to spare him the horror of rotting, and Simon was hiding where she'd never find him. He'd threatened to go underground, and no matter how sick he might become, he was smart.

She nodded. "Let's go." But she didn't move.

She heard gunshots in the distance, and saw smoke rising into the sky. River County hadn't even recovered from COS, and they were being hit again.

The county was going to be destroyed. It was destroying itself.

Jack slid under the wheel, then let down his window.

"Rune. Get in."

She didn't realize Owen was beside her until he took her arm. "Come on."

Rune shook off the melancholy and got into the car. There were more vampires to put down. More babies to save.

Always.

She couldn't afford to wallow in her deep and bloody issues.

The house above the clinic was eerily dark and quiet when they arrived, but that was nothing out of the ordinary. Though the clinic had lost its secrecy in the preceding months, it still maintained its mystery.

Rune walked with Jack and Owen to the front door, the cover door. Her loud knock was not answered, and she closed her eyes for a long second.

"There's some bad shit in there," she said. "Be ready for anything."

She shot out her claws as the other two filled their hands with silver, and with one kick she destroyed the door.

They took the elevator down. Rune placed herself in front of the two men before the doors opened. The elevator spat them out into a clinic that bore little resemblance to the clean, neat place run by Dr. Haas.

The floors were littered with garbage, and the once pristine walls were covered with graffiti. There were no capable nurses hurrying down the hallways, no quiet chimes notifying staff of patient requests.

"What the hell happened here?" Jack murmured.

"Traffickers," Rune replied, keeping her voice low.

"They're using the clinic for headquarters," Owen agreed.

"Then let's find the sons of bitches," Jack said.

They walked quickly but quietly down the hallway, gently nudging open doors to peer into empty rooms. They found no patients.

She cocked her head, almost relieved when the hint of a scream reached her sensitive ears. "I heard a scream, boys. I'm going on ahead. Stay together."

She didn't wait to see if they'd argue, just let her monster free and ran. The clinic was bigger than she'd imagined it would be, with areas she'd never seen.

She half expected the prisoners to be held in the basement, if the clinic had one, but she heard one of them seconds later, locked in an operating room.

The screams came again, louder, more desperate, and Rune hit the doors running. They burst inward, crumbling like crackers.

It took her one horrified minute to process the details—blood, whimpers, the restrained woman, fear…

"My baby," the woman cried. "God, my baby."

Rune knelt on the slippery floor beside her. The woman had delivered recently, and the traffickers had left her on the floor where she'd given birth, her hands cuffed to a table.

She lay in the mess of fluids and blood, her gown shoved up to her waist. "Oh, my baby," she whimpered. Her face was dead pale, her eyes black and feverish. "They took her."

"I know," Rune said. She pushed the woman's sweaty hair out of her face. "I'm going to find your baby."

She broke the chain of the cuffs easily and helped the woman to her feet. When the mother couldn't stand on her own, Rune carried her to one of the tables and placed her carefully on it.

She grabbed Rune's hand. "Don't leave me here. Please, don't leave me here."

"I'll be back. I swear." But she couldn't have pried the desperate grip off her hand without hurting the woman, and she wasn't willing to cause her more pain.

"Fuck me," she said, under her breath, then pulled her cell from her pocket with her free hand.

"I have traffickers and an injured human at the clinic in

Willowburg," she said, when an Annex tech answered. "I need transport here now."

"Are the traffickers neutralized?" he asked.

"They're dead," she said, her voice flat. "That's pretty fucking neutralized."

"Dammit, Alexander," he said. "The boss wanted traffickers brought in alive. We need information, not more dead bodies."

She lifted an eyebrow. "Apologize to Eugene for me. Now get the fucking transport here." She clicked off.

She was in a hurry. She had traffickers to execute.

Jack and Owen stomped into the room, guns and blades ready, death in their hard stares.

"Okay?" Jack asked, gun up.

"They took my baby," the woman cried. "Don't leave me."

"One of you stay with her until the Annex arrives," Rune said. "I called them. I have to find the fucking traffickers and the infant."

Owen glanced once at the tormented woman and headed for the door. "I'll help you search."

Z would have stayed with the woman.

And just that quickly, Rune stopped thinking of Owen as Z.

It hurt. It hurt a lot. It was almost like losing Z all over again. Almost like he died right there in that room. She'd been holding on to him, holding on to him through Owen.

"Rune?" Jack stood beside the woman, gently transferring her grip from Rune's hand to his. "You good?"

She loped toward the doorway, her heart beating wildly, desperate for air. Grief was like that.

It hit her all of a sudden, out of the blue, and tried to send her to her knees.

You going to let me go, sweet thing?

"No," she growled. "Never. *Never*, damn you."

Owen frowned. "Rune?"

"Find me some fucking traffickers," she said, and dropped her fangs with such force they cut her lip.

She didn't wait for his nod before she shot down the hall, her claws slicing through the air, her pain needing an outlet. She needed to cut somebody.

Not herself, though. Not herself.

Just the bad guys.

Her monster ran with her, sniffing the air, more animal than human or even Other, tracking the distinct scent of an infant.

Whatever had softened and hesitated in her since her decapitation hardened once again, manipulated like clay by her monster's strong hands.

She followed the trail through a door that opened into a long, dark hallway. Mingling with the sweet scent of the infant and the sour stench of unwashed humans was the heady perfume of earth and mud and air, and she knew the hallway would lead her to an exit out of the clinic.

She caught them halfway across a back parking lot she hadn't known existed—three men, one carrying a small black duffle bag.

Her monster cracked its knuckles and smiled.

The man carrying the bag threw a look back over his shoulder and screamed, started to run, then turned around and hefted the bag into the air. "Here, here! This is what you want."

She slowed but didn't stop, giving him just enough time to throw the bag at her before she ran her claws through his belly and unzipped him like an ugly dress.

She lowered the bag with its precious contents to the ground, and then she went after the two remaining men.

The one she caught first threw his arms over his head, yelling, "We're not fighters, we're not fighters!" until she silenced him forever.

That left one man, and too bad for him she hadn't gotten the rage out of her system. She stalked him, understanding when he glanced behind her, his eyes showing a flash of hope, that Owen was coming.

Owen.

She wanted to play, but she wanted to kill. Wanted to taste blood. Wanted to be a fucking vicious monster and hurt the asshole who ripped babies from wombs to sell to sick, starving vampires.

She grabbed him, gratified by the terror in his wide eyes. Gratified by his begging.

"Please, please," he moaned. "I'll do anything. I can tell you things—"

"Oh yes," she agreed, "you're going to tell me many things."

She rode him to the ground, to the hard, cold ground, growls coming from her mouth as he fought and struggled and screamed.

She leaned forward and ran her tongue over his lips, sucking on them for a second before putting her mouth on his neck. "You are going to taste so fucking good."

"You're crazy!" he screamed.

"I'm not crazy, baby," she assured him. "I'm mad. There's a difference."

And she slid her fangs into his flesh, soaking up his blood like a dehydrated sponge.

From somewhere behind her, Owen's whisper, full of darkness and delight, floated to her ears.

"Mine…"

CHAPTER TWENTY-THREE

She hadn't realized how unsure she had become until the uncertainty left her. She played with her dinner, coaxing information from him, feeding from him, teasing him with promises of death before finally, she'd taken everything he had to offer.

Replete, she killed him.

She rose from the body, stretching, and caught sight of Owen. He crouched a few yards behind her, watchful. Interested.

She shivered as a chill of danger touched her spine, and then she wiped her mouth with the back of her hand and strolled toward him.

He stood in one smooth movement, his hands loose at his sides, his eyes steady. When she stopped walking he tilted his head, causing his hair to slide silkily over his shoulders, and motioned her on.

But when she didn't move, he did, closing the gap between them. He slid his hand up her arm, over her shoulder, then gripped her neck gently. "In another world," he said, "you're meant for me."

"In this world," she replied, "I'm meant for death."

"Death's mistress," he murmured. "Death isn't always the end."

She reached up to touch his face. "That depends on your definition of end."

"I want to fuck you."

She lost her breath at the ferocity of his words. "I know."

"You just ate a fucking man," he said. "And all I could think was how hot you looked doing it. I got hard watching you suck blood from a guy's neck. I wanted to fuck you while watching you become a monster." He took another step closer, pressing his body against hers. "I wanted you as you killed. What does that make me, Rune Alexander?"

His intensity called to her.

The dark pain in his eyes called to her.

Everything about him called to her.

"I don't fucking know," she whispered.

The baby's cry interrupted her, brought her back to earth, made her remember everything the cowboy had shut out for a long, hot moment.

She turned away from him and fell to her knees beside the bag, nearly ripping it apart in her hurry to reach the baby.

It was alive. *She* was alive.

Rune lifted the infant to her chest. "Damn," she said. "She's so small."

Owen took her arm and helped her to her feet. "Let's take it in."

She felt a twinge when she thought of the little black-haired baby she'd likely never see again. "Come on, kid. Let's get you to your mama."

The berserker met them as they walked back inside the building, his sharp stare softening as he took in the naked, bloody infant squalling in Rune's arms.

Denim was beside him.

"I got the baby, Strad," she said.

He nodded, smiling. "The traffickers?"

"Three of them. Dead. But one of them gave up the locations of two more groups before he died."

"And he told us where a nest of vampires is hiding out

today," Owen said.

Strad looked at him, finally, and Rune felt her heart stop.

She knew death when she saw it, and there was death in the berserker's eyes. There was no doubt at all in his mind that he would kill Owen.

And there was no doubt in hers that he would succeed.

He was the berserker.

In this world I'm meant for Death.

She handed the baby to Denim.

"Owen," she said. "You and Denim take the child inside and wait for transport."

Once they were gone, she looked at Strad. "Why do you want him dead? You kicked the shit out of him already. You made your point. Why do you have such a need to kill him?"

Because maybe she hadn't truly believed, until that moment, that he really would.

"Rune." He closed his eyes and blew out a hard breath, then looked at her. "He will hurt you. You can't see it, but I can. He wants to take you away. To own you. He wants to possess you like a fucking toy. To *hurt* you. And I won't allow it." He shook his head. "I can't."

She squeezed his forearm. "And you think I *would* allow it?" She grinned up at him.

"Oh, sweetheart." He didn't smile and there was only pain in his gaze. "You would. That's who you are."

An image of Jeremy slicing into her flesh, beating her, torturing her, flashed through her mind and she took a quick step back. "Fuck you," she snarled, but she wasn't really talking to the berserker.

He said nothing.

She waited for her heart to slow, to beat a little less painfully.

"What makes you think you know what Owen wants?" she asked, her voice hard.

"There's a little of Owen inside all of us."

"I don't need you to protect me from the fucking cowboy."

His laugh was sharp. "You could crush Owen if you wanted to. I'm not protecting you from him. I'm protecting you from you."

"I'm sick of both of you," she said, suddenly tired. She started to walk away, then turned back. "If you kill him, I won't forgive you."

He kept his stare on hers, and though she saw the hint of a flinch in his eyes, his voice was calm. "I'll do what I have to do."

"So will I."

He nodded. "I know."

She sighed. "You're so fucking…" then she paused. "You're *afraid* of him. You're afraid of Owen."

He stared over her head, silent.

"Strad?"

"Damn you, Rune. I'm afraid of what he can do." He grabbed her upper arms, his grip hard.

"Rune," Levi called, running down the hall. "Hurry."

"Shit," she said, and ran, with Strad right behind her, to meet Levi. "Tell me."

His eyes were too wide, his voice breathless. "Karin Love is at the Annex with an army of COS. She's after Lex."

CHAPTER TWENTY-FOUR

Shiv Crew made it to the Annex without killing anyone, though they broke every speed limit posted getting there.

Lex would be fucking terrified.

They'd thought Karin was away, trapped with Orson Blackthorne, maybe, or sticking close to Damascus.

Obviously they'd been wrong.

Karin Love led her slayers in a battle against the Annex, and the building, along with the people inside it, was being hammered like a dollhouse in a hailstorm.

Fighters burst through doors and spilled out into parking lots, yells of rage mixing with screams of pain, gunfire, and clinks of blades.

The crew slammed their cars to screeching halts in the street and jumped from their vehicles, guns up and blades ready.

"Berserker," Rune screamed, not looking around for him but knowing he'd hear—and heed—her words. "With the twins." The twins were going to need him.

She ran with her claws out, cutting down slayers as she went. She had to get to Lex, and any slayer that got between her and the sick Other was dead.

She didn't see Karin.

A slayer got into her path and maybe it was the way his eyes looked or the color of his hair or just the fact that he was a fucking slayer—she flashed to her time at their mercy, to her pain, to her fear, and it stopped her in her tracks.

He might have put a bullet into her brain had it not been for Owen, who appeared suddenly at her side and sent a blade into the slayers throat.

Then she was back, the split second memory hidden once more beneath the urgency of the fight.

She was pretty sure Eugene would have had himself and Lex spirited to a safe room, but he may not have had time. She had no idea if some of the slayers had managed to slip past Annex guards.

The Annex ops fought like the trained army they were, using long blades, axes, whatever weapon they favored, to put down slayers. Still, they'd been taken by surprise and the slayers would be desperate not to displease Karin.

Shiv Crew, lethal in close combat, fought like two armies.

And they began to take the slayers down.

As the groups thinned out and those slayers still living fell back, Karin Love made her appearance. She stood atop one of the parked cars, unafraid, her voice strong. "Stop," she called, sounding almost bored, and her slayers didn't even hesitate. They stopped fighting immediately—so suddenly most of them died as the Annex ops and Shiv Crew continued the fight.

Karin sought Rune with her cold, black stare. "If you want my daughter to live, you'll take me to her." She gestured at the few slayers remaining. "If my men weren't so worthless I'd have already gained access to her. I can see that won't happen today—but Alexis is running out of time. Take me to her." She shrugged. "Or bring her to me."

Rune stiffened and prepared to race to the COS leader and fling her bloody and screaming into hell.

But she knew she couldn't kill Karin—that was Lex's right. That didn't mean she wouldn't capture the bitch.

"You'll never get one of mine," Rune called.

"Yours?" Karin's mocking laughter was loud in the silence. "She's not *yours*."

Her guard fanned out around the car upon which she stood, guns trained on the crowd. "She's mine. And I am the only person who can cure her." She grinned, looking, for one heart stopping second, so much like Lex that Rune couldn't breathe. "Lex is dying," she continued. "She needs to be with her mama."

The slayers continued backing away, trying to leave the area while their mistress held the attention of their enemies.

Rune wasn't having it. Karin might be able to order the slayers to stop fighting, but she wasn't commanding Shiv Crew. "First we'll kill your slayers," she said, "then we'll take you to Lex."

The crew didn't hesitate. They slaughtered the remaining COS members, their hatred of COS strong, their rage not even remotely assuaged.

The Annex ops joined in, catching and executing fleeing slayers, killing with a grim ferocity that made Rune proud to fight with them.

Karin didn't seem to care that her army was being destroyed. She didn't say another word until only she and her guard remained.

Rune looked up at her. The area was suddenly and completely silent. Even the cops who'd arrived silenced their screaming sirens and watched in silence.

It was surreal, staring up at the most hated enemy she'd ever known, dead littering the ground, lights from cruisers flashing…

The adrenalin from the battle fled and left Rune facing the reality of a fear much worse than spilled blood and battling slayers.

Karin had something planned. She might have believed Rune would take her to Lex before she'd let the little Other die, but Rune wasn't so sure.

No. She had something else.

And then Rune discovered what that was.

"I have your friend. I have Ellis. You really shouldn't have left that poor boy unprotected, Rune. Tsk, tsk." She laughed, lightly, happily. "I'm going to ask Levi to decide. Ellis or Lex?"

Rune's legs weakened and began to shake. Beside her, Levi cried out. She barely heard him over the noise in her head.

"My sweet Levi," Karin said. "What a quandary this must present to you. You love Lex and are fucking Rune's little friend. Whew. I wouldn't want to be you right now."

"I'll get him back," Rune said, her voice hoarse.

"Get him back?" Karin laughed. "You can't get him back from Satan's clutches, lovely Rune. And if you don't agree to go pluck Lex from wherever she'd hiding like a fucking coward, I'm going to send Ellis to hell right now. You have three seconds to agree."

"No," Rune said, despairing. "Karin, don't."

"Give her to me," Karin screamed, suddenly, viciously angry. "Give her *to* me!"

"I'm giving you my monster," Rune muttered, and ran.

Karin's guard opened fire, but their bullets might as well have been bee stings. Rune felt nothing. In her mind, there was only white noise.

Some part of her understood the slayers were shooting into the crowd around her—the Annex ops and her crew.

But even that didn't stop her.

She wanted Karin Love, and she was going to get her.

She tossed Karin's guard out of her way as they shot her pointblank, or tried to. She was fast. She was enraged.

She leaped to the top of the car and hit Karin like a train, sending the other woman through the air. She thought she heard bones crunch as Karin crashed to the pavement below.

As Karin lay battered on the ground trying to remember how to breathe, Rune stood over her, trying to remember how to think.

Ellie.

Karin had him stashed away somewhere, and she'd never trade him for Lex. No matter what she said, Ellie was...

No. No.

Finally, Karin was able to speak. "You'll bring hell down on your world if you kill me."

"We live in hell, asshole. We're used to it." And before Karin could say another word, Rune dragged the woman to her feet. "The end."

"I underestimated you," Karin said, still showing no fear. "I never thought you'd kill one of yours for one of mine."

"Bitch," Rune said, "I told you. Lex isn't yours. Lex is *mine*."

"And Ellis? You'll let him die to keep Lex from me?"

Rune ignored her and pushed the woman through the milling Annex Ops. She was taking Karin to Lex, as she'd promised.

Lex needed to see her mother. She needed to kill her.

Once and for all.

The berserker was suddenly beside her. "I kept one of them alive."

She nodded. She'd known he would. No slayer would keep Karin's secrets when the berserker was torturing them out of him. "Let me know the *second* you find Ellie's location."

Karin laughed.

The rest of the crew walked behind Rune and Karin. Even the twins. They'd stay with Lex. They'd help her do what she needed to do. What all three of them needed to do.

As soon as they entered the building, Karin jerked free of Rune's grip with a sudden, surprising ferocity, nearly ripping Rune's fingernails off, and sprinted down the hall.

Rune overtook her in seconds. She threw her to the floor and almost casually stomped the malevolent woman's ankles, first one and then the other, shattering them. She ignored Karin's screams and looked at Raze. "Carry it."

He dragged Karin off the floor and tossed her over his shoulder.

When she wouldn't stop screaming and struggling and biting, Owen tapped her skull with the butt of his gun.

And at last, there was silence.

CHAPTER TWENTY-FIVE

Eugene stood in the hallway with five men at his back, blocking her path. His face was pale, his eyes as black as cigarette burns in an old couch. He looked only at Rune. "I need her, Rune. She's too valuable for you to kill."

Anger flared, and just as quickly fled. "I'm taking her to Lex, Eugene. Don't try to stop me." Her voice was toneless.

"You can have her when I've finished with her," he said.

She became aware, slowly, of the anguish in his eyes. "What has she done to you?" she asked him.

He tightened his lips. "Most of the people in this building and all the Others in this town have been affected by Karin Love."

"Not the way Lex was affected," Denim snarled. "Not even close."

Levi said nothing, surely tormented by thoughts of his love in the hands of COS.

"Move your men out of my way, Eugene," Rune said.

"You will kill Karin," he snapped, "and allow Ellis to die?"

She flinched. "She won't tell me where he is no matter what we do. You know that."

"But I can get the cure out of her," he said. "I can save the Others with this woman. It's not just about Lex,

Rune."

"Move out of our way," Jack said. "If you get this hag, she'll escape, she'll live, and she'll go on to torment the world." He took a step forward, slightly in front of Rune. "*That* is what will happen. You won't get your cure and we won't get Ellis's location. That's the truth."

"Back away," Eugene said.

The ops at Eugene's back lifted their guns and trained them on Jack, but he ignored them. "You'll leave Rune the fuck alone."

But Rune turned her head slowly to look at him. "Jack," she said. "What if he *can* get the antidote? What if he can get Ellie's location?"

What if she didn't have to go to Skyll?

"Let's take her to Lex," Raze said. "At least let her be in on the decision. Maybe she can touch this garbage and get the information that way."

Rune put her hand to her chest. "Fuck me," she exclaimed. "Of course. Why *wouldn't* Lex be able to read her?"

She started toward Eugene's men, hopeful. "Eugene. I'm taking this bitch to Lex. Get your boys out of my way or I'll drop them where they stand."

Lex could do what torture couldn't. She could read nearly anyone by touching them. She could surely read her bitch of a mother.

Karin had regained consciousness but kept her mouth shut. Maybe she didn't want another concussion.

Eugene waved his men away, a gleam of hope in his eyes.

"Where are Bill and Elizabeth?" Rune asked him as they made their way down the hall.

"My ops took Elizabeth and Fie to a safe room. Bill has been unreachable for the last three hours." He glanced at her, silently reminding her of her agreement to follow Bill.

"One disaster at a time," she murmured.

Before they reached Lex's room, three ops came from

the opposite direction, pushing Lex in a wheelchair.

"Hang back," Rune told Raze. "Knock her out again if she opens her mouth."

Jack took the wheelchair from the ops, then pushed Lex into her room.

"What happened?" Lex asked. "No one would tell me anything."

Her eyes were sluggish, listless. Her skin was so hot it had begun to split and peel.

And wafting from her was just the slightest hint of the ripe, unimaginable scent characteristic of those with the disease.

She had no idea Karin was near, and that scared the hell out of Rune. Lex was worsening quickly, and if her abilities were compromised, she might not be able to read her mother.

Rune knelt down beside the chair and took Lex's hands in hers. "Do you want me to feed you?"

Lex wet her lips. "No. It wouldn't help. I can feel the rot spreading through me. It's a bad feeling, Rune."

Rune closed her eyes. "I'm so sorry, Lex."

"Are you sick? Do you feel it?"

"No. Not yet."

"Super Rune," Lex whispered. "Holder of demons and berserkers."

"And cowboys," Owen murmured.

Rune didn't glance at him. "Karin is our prisoner," she blurted. "I have her. I need to know what you want to do with her. She's captured Ellis and I don't know where he is." And as she said it, it became more real. "God. She has Ellie."

Lex tilted her head, too dazed to fully comprehend Rune's words. "What?"

"Raze is holding her out in the hallway," Eugene said. "Karin attacked the Annex and we've captured her. She claims she knows of the cure to the rotting disease."

"And Ellis's location," Rune said. "We need that, Lex.

Can you read her?"

"Oh," Lex said, and leaned over to rest her forehead on the chair arm. "She's here. It's too late, then."

Rune's stomach tightened. "Lex?"

Lex straightened. "If she's here, it's because she wants to be here."

The crew looked at each other.

"She came after you, baby."

"I can't think," Lex said. "My head hurts so much."

"Can you read her if we bring her in?" Eugene asked, impatient.

"I can try," Lex said, but she shuddered. "Don't leave me alone with her."

"Never," Rune said. She squeezed Lex's hand. "We'll all be right here."

"Lex," Eugene said, putting a hand on the Other's shoulder. "If you can't read her, I'll need to secure her and see if my specialists can get the information from her. Is that okay?"

"She'll never die," Lex said.

"She's not immortal." Rune stood, but continued holding Lex's hand. "I can kill her, I promise you."

"But I need to…talk with her before you kill her," Eugene said. "The crew wants you to agree to that before I take her."

"You won't get anything out of her," Lex said. "No matter what you do. And if anyone is going to try to kill her, it'll be me and the twins. Bring her to me." She released Rune's hand. "I'll read her. For Ellie."

Rune pushed her fist against her stomach.

Ellie.

She left the room, dread lying like a rock in her stomach.

"Lex okay?" Raze asked, when she reached him.

Karin sat on the floor, her broken ankles out before her, hands fastened behind her with zip ties. She watched Rune calmly.

Rune stared down at the woman. "She's up to something."

Raze shrugged. "Maybe she had an agenda other than getting Lex, but it doesn't matter. We have *her*. One way or another she dies tonight."

Rune nodded, relieved to see a little spark of uncertainty in Karin's eyes. Rune wasn't going to kill her right then, but Karin couldn't know that. "The end of fucking Karin Love."

She couldn't contain herself at the thought, at the reality of it, and shot out her claws.

"If you kill me, you'll never find out where your friend is," Karin said.

Rune leaned over and put a claw to Karin's throat. "You won't tell me anyway, and I *really* want to see your blood on the floor."

"I'll tell you," Karin said. "I'll tell you, monster, because there's nothing you can do about it."

Rune straightened, her heartbeat so strong it hurt her healed stake wounds. "Tell me," she whispered.

Karin pursed her lips, then shook her head. "I was just fucking with you. I'll never tell." She grinned.

Rage ripped through Rune, clawing her insides, screaming to be released. And it wasn't just that Karin had Ellie. It was that Karin was calm and unafraid and Rune wanted her to suffer more than she'd ever wanted anything else in her life.

So she sliced through Karin's eyes.

Karin's screams didn't really make her feel any better. She grabbed Karin by her hair and jerked her head back. "Now you know how Lex felt when you blinded her."

Only Karin would never know, not really, because Lex had been a child. Unprotected, unloved, abused. Karin was a horrific adult who knew the way the world worked.

She felt the pain, and perhaps she felt some terror at having her sight stolen from her. But she would never feel what Lex had felt.

Eugene rushed down the hall. "Rune," he yelled. "You're not to kill her."

"I didn't kill her," Rune said, but she was shaking from the effort it took her not to finish Karin right then and there.

Eugene took her arm and urged her away.

"Bring that thing to Lex," he told Raze.

So Raze grabbed the hysterical, injured woman by her collar and dragged her down the hallway, while Rune watched with claws ready and suspicion in her heart.

Ten seconds later they entered the room with Karin, and Lex began to scream.

CHAPTER TWENTY-SIX

"Lex," Rune said, grabbing her shoulders. "She can't hurt you."

Owen stood at the girl's back, his blades out as he prepared for trouble. Levi and Denim wanted to shrink away, wanted to run from the room and get as far away from Karin as possible—Rune could see it in their faces.

But they stayed put, tall, brave sentinels watching over their little Other.

Lex quieted, slowly, shuddering. "She's here."

"Lex," Karin cried. "They hurt me. Oh God, baby, they hurt me."

Lex sobbed, a heartbreaking sound that must have echoed throughout the building. Maybe, Rune thought, it echoed throughout the world.

The pain and fear in her cries were overwhelming to those who loved her.

But worse than that was the need in her voice. No matter what her mother had done to her, she still, somewhere deep inside, wanted to know why. Wanted, even, the love that had been withheld from her.

Maybe she even hurt for Karin.

"Lex," Levi cried. "Don't. Don't…"

Don't hurt.

Don't cry.

But Lex could not be consoled. "I'd rather die," she

said, her sobs dwindling to weak whimpers. "I'd rather die. I can't stand the pain."

The twins held her, Raze stood like a stone, frozen and helpless, and Owen waited with unreadable eyes to see how it would all play out.

Rune wanted to take Lex's hand and wrap it around Karin's wrist, but nothing could have forced her to be the one to make that move.

It was too cruel.

Eugene did it for her. "Cut her restraints," he told Raze.

The moment Lex's fingers made contact with her mother's wrist, the little Other's entire body stiffened. With her hand still attached to Karin's arm, she flung herself backward so violently that the chair moved.

"No," she screamed, a long, drawn-out howl of anguish that let the others know, finally, that she wanted free of her mother.

But she couldn't pry herself loose.

Raze grabbed Karin by her arm and tried to yank her away from Lex, but it was as though the two were glued together with something even stronger than Raze, and they couldn't be forced apart.

Lex's eyes began to bleed.

Blood leaked from the corners of her mouth, her nose, her ears.

And she continued to scream.

Rune didn't think—she couldn't think over the terror inside Lex's screams. She fought through the fog in her mind, shot out her claws, and sliced off Karin Love's head.

The twins dragged Lex from the chair and fell to the floor with her, their arms wrapped around her, trying to protect her from whatever horror her mother had forced her to see.

It was in the midst of that chaotic mess that Strad burst into the room, his spear out, eyes wild. He speared Karin's headless body, right through the heart, as though he didn't at first realize the woman was dead.

Rune backed away and closed her eyes, trying to shut out the sounds and agony and the overwhelming, dismal feeling that once again, the wrong choices had been made.

Lex stopped screaming all at once, but the blood continued gushing from her body. She opened her mouth and all that came out was a crimson rush.

Somehow, Karin Love had managed to do exactly what she'd wanted.

She'd killed Lex.

Rune felt hands on her shoulders and turned. "Strad. It was a mistake."

He nodded. "Karin never had Ellis."

"What?" She grabbed his huge arms, unable to believe she'd heard him right. "What?"

"Ellis is on his way in. He'd gone with his mother to Columbus hours ago. I had someone check, and your house was broken into. COS had planned to take Ellis, but he wasn't home." He leaned down to peer into her eyes. "Our Ellis is *safe*, Rune."

"And when they told Karin he wasn't there, she went ahead with her plans as though she had him," Jack guessed.

"She was in a hurry," Owen said, from behind the berserker.

"Karin…"

"Needed to be taken to Lex, and she couldn't wait."

Rune wanted to fall to the floor, wanted to cry, to rage, to bring Karin back to life so she could kill her again.

She only nodded.

Karin had fucked them all.

Since she'd ended up dead, none of them knew why.

Rune walked to where the twins huddled around Lex and knelt down beside the three of them. "Ellis is fine," she told Levi. "Karin didn't have him. He's on his way here."

He closed his eyes and nodded.

"Lex," Rune said. She pulled Lex's hand to her arm. "Read me. You're okay. Karin is dead."

Lex lay against Denim's chest, her eyes closed, her lips parted. She breathed shallowly, but her bleeding had slowed to a trickle.

She didn't tighten her fingers around Rune's arm, didn't acknowledge her in any way. Lex wasn't there.

"None of us can bear to lose you," Rune whispered. "Please, Lex. Come back."

"She's so sick," Denim said. "Karin made it worse."

"Karin made everything worse," Levi said.

Then the twins looked at each other. "Karin's dead," they said, at the exact same time.

Rune glanced at the body. Eugene had already called techs to take it out, to take it, likely, to a lab where they could study her remains in hopes of finding something helpful.

He looked at Rune. "Anything?"

"She can't talk yet," Rune said. "I'll let you know."

He nodded and left the room behind the techs who'd zipped Karin and her head into a white bag and hauled her away.

"She's gone," Rune told the twins. "Finally. She can't hurt you anymore."

Lex laughed.

The laugh, weak and gurgling though it was, sent chills down Rune's spine. "Lex?"

Lex tried to sit up, but fell back, too weak. She groaned. "She's got me. She's got me now."

Rune began to shiver and couldn't stop.

She's got me. She's got me now.

"Karin's dead," she said, almost angrily. "I killed the bitch."

Lex said nothing.

It'd been too easy. Karin Love would never go easily, and it'd been too fucking easy.

"Shit," Rune said. "Could she really have wanted us to

kill her?"

"Better question," Jack said. "How do we fight a fucking ghost?"

"What does she want, Lex?" Strad took Lex's hand. "Why would she want to die?"

"I don't know," Lex muttered. "I'm going to be sick. Give me a bag."

Raze yanked a green plastic bag from the side table and hurried it to the blind Other. "Here."

But Lex didn't throw up. She passed out.

Ellis hurried into the room. "I'm here."

Levi jumped to his feet and raced to Ellis. He dragged Ellie into his arms, his breathing ragged. "God," he said. "God, Ellie."

Rune sat on the floor, needing to regroup, but unable to manage. There were too many questions. Too much confusion.

Karin was dead, but she hadn't gone without a good fucking reason.

Lex was dying.

And Rune had to go to another world to save her. To save all the Others.

To limbus, limbo, Skyll.

To Damascus.

Damascus was her Karin.

But she'd sell her soul to Damascus if doing so would save Lex.

It was time to listen, really listen, for the echoes.

Part Three

THE ECHOES

CHAPTER TWENTY-SEVEN

She had to go home, to disengage, just for a little while.
If that made her weak, that was okay.
She wasn't the only one. All the crew went home—most of them to her house to crash until…
Until when the fuck ever.
She took Lex with her.
The girl needed to be with the ones who loved her, not in a hospital bed surrounded by white walls and machines.
Lex didn't talk much. Her subdued behavior wasn't unusual. She was sick, and she'd just faced a mother who'd tortured her childhood and haunted her nightmares.
A mother who'd just died.
But Rune was uneasy.
Something was wrong. It was just a matter of time before whatever it was came roaring out of hiding to kick all their asses.
After she got some sleep, she was going to Wormwood to listen for the echoes. Gunnar had assured her she didn't need to be in the graveyard, but she knew she did.
Her crew was going with her. That was their choice.
A choice she wasn't arguing with.
But that was for later.
Right then, she had Strad Matheson to focus on.
She barely waited for him to close the bedroom door before she started yanking blades from sheaths, kicking off

her boots, tearing off her clothes.

She was wound too tightly to be careful, but she didn't need to be careful with the berserker. He could take what she needed to give him.

And he could give it back.

Neither of them said anything. There was nothing to say and everything to feel.

She kissed his wounds, then tore them open with her eagerness. Her urgency made her afraid, because her gut…

Her gut was telling her bad things were coming.

The berserker would make her forget her gut.

For a little while.

They were running out of time.

She felt it.

"Rune," he said, only once, pulling away to look down at her, his eyes glassy, almost black, like tiny ponds frozen over with ice.

"Yes," she cried, digging her fingers into his sides. "Don't hold back. You know what I need. Be the fucking berserker for me."

Maybe he, too, sensed the urgency, because for the first time, he showed her what the berserker unleased was like in bed.

She thought she knew.

She didn't.

Once, Ellis came to the door, knocking. "Rune? Are you okay? Rune?"

She couldn't answer but heard the calm tones of Owen's voice as he reassured Ellis and pulled him away from the door.

The same moment she heard Owen's voice, Strad drove himself inside her and pushed her mouth against his throat.

She bit him…

And they were connected, the three of them, somehow.

Owen's voice echoed through her mind, caressing her insides, sending long frosty fingers down her spine, touching her.

Strad battered her body, fucked her, hurt her in a way she needed to be hurt.

And she drank.

"Trust me…"

Her orgasm started and didn't stop. It shook her entire body, her brain, her heart.

She screamed, maybe, as the enormity of that orgasm held her prisoner, became too much, and refused to ease.

"When you're fucking him, remember how it feels to want me."

And then, finally…

"How did I forget?"

Words, hiding thoughts, hiding echoes.

They were there.

She felt them, heard them, because she knew she should. She recognized them. But she wasn't ready for them.

Just as she'd *never* been ready for them.

So she pretended not to know what the voices that weren't really voices were. She shut them out.

And the echoes faded.

She lay on Strad's chest, her hair tangling with his, her fingers digging into his flesh. He was there, warm and real.

She shuddered.

"You okay?" he asked. His voice was hoarse, his arms lying heavy at his sides. He didn't move.

No. "Yeah. You?"

He didn't answer.

She summoned the strength to roll off him. It took another two minutes before she could move again.

He was wounded—new wounds mixed with his battle wounds and the wounds he'd sustained during his capture.

But none of those wounds would kill him.

He didn't look at her.

She frowned, stretching out her muscles as her body became stronger. "Strad?"

They'd gone into the darkness together. She

understood he wasn't going to be happy about that.

His throat clicked as he swallowed. "I fucked you up."

"I've been fucked up since birth, baby." She kept her tone light and slid her fingers over his ribs. "You had nothing to do with it."

Yeah, he'd hurt her.

"Rune."

"Don't get all guilt-ridden and shit, Strad. I asked you to be the berserker."

"I told you I can't be that kind of help."

She shrugged, then flinched. "You're not Jeremy. It's nothing like that." She smiled, though he wasn't looking at her, and ran her thumb over his nipple. "I like rough sex."

"If you were human you'd be dead."

"But I'm not human. And you're not Jeremy." She'd keep saying it until he believed it. Because it was true.

"What the fuck did he do to you, Rune?"

She pushed herself up and waited for him to look at her. "He hated me, is what he did. He hated me as much as I hated myself." She leaned over and licked the blood smeared across his cheek. "I gave him nothing back. I let him restrain me and I let him beat the fuck out of my monster. I let him shame me, punish me, hurt me. Because I wanted to be hurt that way. I wanted to pay for killing my parents. I wanted someone to punish me for being a fucking monster. I don't anymore."

He said nothing, just stared up at her.

"And now," she continued, "my monster could tear apart these walls and use the wood for toothpicks. I need you to be *you* with me. All of you."

He smiled, sort of. "I know what you need, sweetheart. But I don't want any part of me or what I do to be anything like what he was or what he did to you."

"Shit was muddled with Jeremy. I was a mess of need and sickness and hatred." She shook her head. "That's not what this is."

When he remained silent she shrugged again. It felt

good, just the tiniest hint of pain. "This was rough sex. Sex for a monster. I can take anything you give me, Berserker. And I can like it."

But she knew without a doubt that the berserker was going to kick himself for hurting her, even though in the heat of the moment he hadn't been able to care.

CHAPTER TWENTY-EIGHT

"I heard the echoes," she told Gunnar, as they walked through Wormwood. The crew had gone to work, and though she should have been there as well, she needed first to talk to the ghoul.

Dawn was absent, and the graveyard was silent.

It seemed even more vast than usual. The old tombstones were familiar, but the air was stagnant and dry. For a moment, she had the eerie feeling that she and Gunnar were alone in the cemetery.

The Others were dying off.

"Yet you are still here," he said.

"I'm not sure how to go." But she heard the lie in her voice. She hadn't wanted to go, and it was as simple as that. "I'll hear them again."

"Perhaps."

"I'll fix this, Gunnar."

"You're the only one who can, Your Highness."

She clenched her fists, suddenly angry. "And why the fuck *is* that?"

He turned toward her, his cheekbones sharper than ever, his eyes sunken. "No human can cross over to Skyll, Rune. Unless that human is dead, the worlds have aligned at the perfect moment, and the human is sucked in." He started to touch her arm, then quickly withdrew his hand. "No human can go. Do you understand?"

Her legs shook and she had to concentrate on nothing to keep standing. "It means my crew can't go with me. That's what it means."

He nodded. "Humans cannot pass the barrier, coming or going. You must go alone. And you *must* return."

"To save the world," she mumbled, still shocked, but some part of her not surprised.

"To save the Others," he said.

"But we were in that world," she told him. "When we went to Orson Blackthorne's lab. They were with me then."

"You were on a path, dear. You were not in Skyll."

She swallowed her arguments. He knew more about it than she did. "What can you tell me? What do I need to know about that place?"

"It will not be easy."

"Yeah, I kind of already figured that one out for myself, sexy. What else you got?"

"You will see familiar faces. Nothing there is as it is here. It is a world made up of magic. Others rule. There are no laws except the ones created by those in power to suit themselves and torture the lowers. You will see. All I can tell you is that you can return. When you doubt yourself, remember how weak old Gunnar brought back his ghoul friend."

She grinned despite herself. "Ghoul friend."

He looked at her, stern. "You cannot fail. Keep that as your truth."

"I cannot, Gunnar?"

He hesitated. "You will not."

She sighed, but was less afraid. She no longer had to wonder if taking her crew was a bad idea. She no longer had to worry that Skyll would kill them. They weren't going. And though she would have to go alone to face Damascus, she was relieved.

But when they found out, every one of her crew was going to be upset.

It was time to ask the question she really doubted the ghoul had the answers to. Or maybe she was just afraid he'd tell her it was all a lie. That Strad hadn't been taken. That Dawn hadn't killed his guards.

That he'd lied to her.

"Who held the berserker, Gunnar?"

"I did not know them. I would have left them to their business but Dawn insisted we rescue that one. For you." He lifted an eyebrow.

"You must know something about it. You know a little about every other thing that goes on around here."

"I suspect their motives, but I do not know who they were. I do not know the ones who commanded them."

"Motives?" She crossed her arms. "What motives?"

"He would convince you not to go to Skyll."

She frowned. "Someone took Strad because they were afraid he'd keep me from finding a cure for the Others?"

He shrugged. "Perhaps they were simply afraid he would keep you from going. You are wanted there, Rune. By many. That is all I have for you—and that could be an incorrect assumption."

"Why now?"

"Because now is the time." He lifted an eyebrow. "*I* do not hold the secrets of the worlds."

"You seem to hold more than your share, ghoul."

She couldn't convince him to smile.

"You're worried about me," she said.

He looked over her head, his gaze distant. "I have always worried about you, Your Cherishedness."

"Always, Gunnar? That's a long time."

"Yes," he agreed. "It is forever."

She hated that he was solemn, sad, desolate. Hated that he knew or felt things she couldn't understand. Mostly she hated that she couldn't help him.

"It'll be okay," she told him, grabbing his long fingers and squeezing his hand. "I'll bring back the antidote for the Others. For you, and Lex…"

She let him pull away as she realized something.

"Lex," she murmured. "I can take Lex." She focused on the ghoul's long face. "I can take Lex, Gunnar?"

"Maybe. You can try." He shook his head and his long, fluffy hair drifted aimlessly about his head. "But perhaps you should not."

"Because she's sick? Because it's too dangerous?"

He tilted his head. "Both those things are true. But I fear she will not want to return with you. And I would not see you heartbroken."

"The wasteland. It was familiar. I think my father came from there. I could see. In the…tunnel, or whatever it was—the path. I could see in there."

Hadn't she known, when they were on the path, that Lex would need to go? That she would believe she belonged there?

Maybe she *did* belong there.

But Rune wasn't sure she could let her have the chance to decide.

"Lex is dying," she told Gunnar. "She's not strong."

"She may not last until your return," he agreed.

Rune closed her eyes. "God. What should I do?"

"You must decide that for yourself." He leaned toward her suddenly. "You are sick as well."

"I know," she admitted.

"You have time. But without the cure you will become…"

"A brain in a jar," she finished.

He thought about it, then nodded. "Yes. But don't fret. If that were to happen, you would still be here in spirit. And your men will build an exquisite shelf on which your jar might perch."

She gaped. "Fuck you, ghoul."

And finally, he smiled.

"Go away," he said. "The echoes will sound again."

She studied him for a long moment. "What's the other reason you risked yourself to fetch Dawn? It wasn't just to encourage me, was it?"

He pursed his lips. "Some things are not your concern, Your Horror." He ambled away, patting gently the coat pocket holding his candy.

So she left Wormwood with more questions than when she'd arrived.

There were things to wrap up before she left.

When she walked into the Annex and saw Bill talking with two younger employees, she stopped to watch him.

He looked like shit. He'd lost weight, his skin was sallow, his eyes dull. He had a new bruise on his cheekbone, and when at last he hefted his briefcase and marched away from the other two men, he limped.

Just slightly, but she noticed.

Someone was beating the hell out of him.

And he was too afraid or too proud to get help.

Rage hit her all at once, choking her. She strode toward him, but before she reached him Eugene headed her off.

"No," he said.

She looked at him, too angry to speak.

"Follow him, Rune. Berating him, nagging him, that will only make him close up further. Follow him and don't stop until you find out what's going on."

She gave him a curt nod and went to find her crew.

But that night, one way or the other, she was finding out what the *fuck* was happening to Bill Rice.

CHAPTER TWENTY-NINE

"Where's Raze?" Rune and the crew were ready to leave the Annex and get to work. She paced restlessly, eager to release a little nervous energy. But not without Raze.

"He went back to check on Lex," Levi said. "I've texted him our locations and he'll meet us there."

Rune nodded.

Raze's love of the little Other was no secret. The only thing that would keep him calm when—if—Lex left Spiritgrove with Rune was the realization that it would save her life.

Unless it killed her.

They spent the day fighting, invading nests of traffickers, and putting down diseased Others.

Each time they found a trafficker, he was more than willing to turn in another trafficker in return for his life.

And each time Rune prepared to kill him anyway, he seemed genuinely shocked that she wasn't going to hold up her end of the bargain.

As if.

But no matter what they did that day, it didn't calm the restlessness inside her. It didn't settle her.

Her mind was focused on leaving her crew. On *telling* her crew. On the unknown that awaited her.

The twins and Strad would suffer without her—that

was a cruel fact of the addiction. There wasn't anything at all she could do about it—except take care of business in Skyll and get the fuck back to her people.

The berserker would tear Wormwood apart searching for a way in. He wouldn't believe traveling to Skyll was impossible until he proved it to himself.

She had to talk to her crew, and she had to take Lex to Wormwood.

Because even if the echoes were inside her, she would hear them better if they were in the cemetery, not at home watching the crew's worried faces.

The sun was setting when she and the crew finished their debriefings and left the Annex building to head home. She halted at her car door and turned to her men, not surprised when they all gathered automatically around her.

They knew her. They knew something was coming.

She cleared her throat.

"Say it, Rune," Jack said.

"I can't take you with me when I'm…" she gestured. "Sucked into limbo."

Strad crossed his arms. "We're going."

"You can't go. It's not that I won't take you. I *can't*. Only the odd dead human can slip into Skyll. Dead humans and some Others. And you all are neither."

"Then you won't go," he said.

"She has to go," Raze said. "It's the only way she can save the Others. And Lex."

The twins looked at each other. "Okay," Denim murmured.

"I'm taking Lex with me," she said. "If she will go."

For a long moment, no one said anything. The twins opened their mouths, then closed them. Raze clenched his fists.

And finally, they nodded.

"Will you come back?" Jack asked. "I mean, will you really come back?"

"I have to," she answered. "I will."

But she knew she might not.

So did they.

Owen said nothing.

"When?" Jack asked, his voice strained.

"I don't know. I just…don't know. But it has to be soon. I have to figure my shit out *soon*."

Time was running out for all of them.

She could feel the rot. Feel it spreading through her body like ink on paper. She would lose her monster.

Lose her fight.

I'm afraid.

You're everything, sweet thing. You're alive.

No one knew what to do or how to act. Finally, the berserker started to stride away then turned back and grabbed her to him.

"Don't leave me forever," he whispered.

She couldn't speak.

And then there was nothing to do but go home.

Strad tailed her all the way, unwilling to let her out of his sight. As she drove up her street, she called her floater.

"News?" she asked.

"He's been home for three hours and forty-seven minutes. Hasn't so much as looked out a window since."

"Thanks."

And just as she clicked off, Eugene called.

She stiffened automatically at the tenseness in his tone.

"Our killer has left us another body, Rune. He's changed his MO again."

"Fuck. Did you call Bill?"

He hesitated. "I tried. He didn't answer. I'll try to get him again. You'll head out to the scene?"

"Yeah. Give me the location. And after, I'll swing by Bill's house to check on him."

He gave her the location of the latest body—behind an ice cream shop called Missy's in the city. She didn't ask for more information. She'd get more than he had when she got there.

But first…she glanced into her rearview at Strad's car, following her much too closely. She pulled into her drive and jumped out, then strode to the berserker's car window. "I got a call from Eugene. He wants me to check out a murder. Then I'm going to see Bill. I need to do that before I'm…"

"Gone," he finished.

She backed away from the window. "I'll be back tonight. I swear it."

Without hesitating further, she called her monster while it was still hers to call. Using all the considerable speed she possessed, she flew from the Moor.

And suddenly, it felt like the end.

Like she was finishing up, and it was the end.

Whatever sound of agony she made then was snatched away by the wind, and she ran on, her heart a thousand pounds of pain in her chest.

CHAPTER THIRTY

Eugene had sent some of his people to guard the scene until she had a chance to look it over. They maintained a wide but unobtrusive perimeter around the area.

No hue and cry had been raised, no human investigators demanded entry, and no cars with lights pulsing sat in the street.

There were only Annex ops and a sad, destroyed body.

"He's changed his MO again."

Indeed he had.

"What does it mean when a serial killer keeps changing shit up?" she murmured, not expecting an answer, but one of the ops, a young woman Rune vaguely remembered, spoke.

"Maybe he got a late start and is just finding his way."

Rune nodded. "You may be right, Ms. Anderson."

"Sasha, please." She grinned and held out a hand to Rune, then darted a look at the body. "Or maybe our killer just likes to screw with us."

Rune shook the ops hand, then pulled a small flashlight from her pocket. She knelt down beside him and flashed the light over his melted face, then his naked, bludgeoned body. "Or maybe," she said, to herself more than Sasha, "each victim is killed in a way that is personal to him." She eyed the dead man's mutilated genitalia.

"Reflects something that happened to him," Sasha

agreed. "Or to those he loved."

Rune closed her eyes for a long moment, inhaling, trying unsuccessfully to get a scent from the killer. She smelled only blood and charred flesh.

She caught a bit of color beneath his hand and lifted it gently to get at the scrap of purple paper lying on the ground. The edge of it was caught between his fingers.

It was a note—their first real communication from the killer.

Her heart began to beat with slow, heavy thumps.

I am the blade of vengeance for Others who suffered beneath hard human hands.

Shit.

Other. The killer was Other.

And he was right—every one of the victims who could be identified had long histories of criminal activity. But the killer must have known something they didn't if he was sure his victims had done harm to Others.

"Vengeance killer," she muttered.

"A news van is heading this way," one of the other ops told her, his voice quiet, but alert.

"That was fast," Rune said. "Not a word. And keep them back."

She called Eugene and told him what she'd found.

"Bring me the note," he said. "I'm still at the Annex."

She left the dead man to the Annex ops and the humans who'd soon be flooding the area and jogged toward the Annex. An Annex mobile lab was already easing toward the crime scene.

Eugene's eyes sat atop pillows of puffy flesh, and his skin was too pale. "Thank you, Rune," he said, when she handed him the note. "I'll see if we can get some prints off this, but our killer isn't stupid. Or careless."

She gave him a curt nod and turned to leave.

"Elizabeth took Fie to her house," he said.

She frowned and faced him once more. "Was she ready to leave the Annex?"

He shrugged. "I would rather she have stayed, but Elizabeth thought it best to take the child somewhere slightly more…normal. She'll bring her back for testing and for the lengthy stay she'll require after we've built her a face."

"You have ops guarding the house?"

"Of course. No one is getting to the child."

"You shouldn't have let them leave." Rune caressed her stake wounds absentmindedly, stopping when Eugene's stare settled on her fingers.

"I wanted to keep Elizabeth calm, and maybe she's right. Fie was growing very unsettled here. She was unhappy."

And you care about her happiness. Right.

She turned once more to leave, and that time, he didn't stop her.

She toyed briefly with the idea of going home and delaying her talk with Bill, but she ignored her almost overwhelming desire for her bed and berserker and asked an op to drive her to Bill's place. Her boots were shredded from that night's little trek across the pavement.

She called her floater before she got there. "Any movement?"

"None."

"You can take off. I'm on my way there."

"You got it."

Bill's house was completely dark when she arrived. She stared up at it for a full five minutes before she knocked on his front door.

He didn't answer the door until she rang the bell, knocked again, and then texted him threatening to kick the door in.

Finally, the outside light came on, and he opened the door. "What the *fuck* are you doing here this time of night?"

"We need to talk."

"Now?" He ran a hand over his face. "Rune. I told

you—"

"Let me in, Bill."

He blew out a tired breath and motioned her inside. "Be my guest."

She sat down and waited for him to sit across from her before she spoke. "I want to know what's going on with you. I'm not going to let someone I care about be tormented by a nameless asshole. Tell me what's going on." She crossed her arms and leaned back. "I'm not leaving until I get answers."

"Do you want coffee?"

"Do you want to stop delaying?" But hell, she *did* want coffee. "Fuck," she muttered, beneath her breath. She ignored his tiny smile and followed him into the kitchen.

His house was neat and uncluttered with small rooms and matching furniture. There was nothing personal about it. No photos, no pile of magazines or newspapers, no pets. Not even a fake plant or a shelf of knickknacks.

"Your house is too sterile, dude," she said.

He put the coffee on and got two mugs from the cabinet. "I'm rarely home. I sleep here. The rest of the time I'm at work."

"Elizabeth took Fie home."

"I know."

"Not a good idea."

"She's heavily guarded."

"Still. Not a good idea. She was guarded the first time she was taken."

He shrugged. "I'm fucking tired, Rune."

Too tired to care about Fie.

"Bill…"

"Tell me about our serial killer."

So she did.

By the time she'd finished telling him about the events of the night, she was on her third cup of coffee and he appeared a little more relaxed.

"What's going on, Bill?"

He looked down at his empty mug and pushed it back and forth between his palms. "I can't tell you. But you're right. We did need to have this talk. I'm not hurt. I'm not being beaten or attacked or tortured by anyone." He spread his hands and looked at her, and finally, there was the old Bill lurking in his smile. "I am exactly where I need to be, Rune. Stop worrying. And no matter what Eugene says, you don't need to follow me or post floaters outside my house." He leaned closer to her. "If the floater had been an Annex op, I'd have killed him. He lives because he's yours." He sat back. "I'm sure that's why Eugene sent you instead of his people."

She couldn't look at him. "I couldn't let anyone fuck with you."

He reached over to take her hands. "You have to stop thinking that everyone is your responsibility. We have our own lives, and parts of our lives are not Eugene's business. Not *your* business." He softened his voice. "Leave me alone, dear. Please."

He was right. She knew he was right.

And Eugene Parish had sent her to stick her nose—and his—where it didn't belong. She'd spied on a friend. "If you ever need me, I'm here."

Yeah, she felt like shit.

She stood and carried her cup to the sink. Bill said nothing as she rinsed out her mug, and she said nothing as she placed the cup carefully on the countertop and walked from the house, leaving Bill to his secrets, his bruises, and his life.

CHAPTER THIRTY-ONE

When she woke up the next morning, the serial killer had a name.

Vengeance Killer! was stamped on the front pages of newspapers, the talk of the early morning shows, and the highlight of the news programs.

She called Eugene. "One of your ops talked to the media."

"I know." His voice was tight. "It's been handled."

Shit. "I hope it wasn't Sasha. I like that girl."

"How was Bill? He's at work right now but declined to talk with me during this morning's briefing."

"He knows you sent me to spy on him. He even knew about the floater I posted outside his house. He wasn't happy and told me, basically, to fuck off."

"What are you going to do?"

"I'm going to fuck off. So are you."

"Don't think you can—"

"I'm not having this conversation. You and I are going to leave Bill alone. That's the end of it."

"Fine, fine. But I have a feeling you're going to regret that decision."

She hesitated. She didn't have a good track record with making the right decisions. Eugene knew that. He was playing her. "Fuck off," she said, but softly.

"Rune?"

She hung up and turned at Ellie's voice.

His gaze was questioning and held the slightest bit of anxiety. "Are you okay?"

"I'm fine, baby."

"I made breakfast. Come eat before you go in."

She grabbed him to her with a suddenness that startled both of them. "I'd give anything to see you happy again, Ellie."

He pulled far enough away to peer into her eyes. "I'm not unhappy. I'm worried about you. I don't have time to recover from one scare before I'm hit with another." He smiled, and for an instant he looked like the Ellie of old. "I have Levi, and…I realized I've never really been in love before, Rune."

"What's that like, Ellie?"

He widened his eyes and stared at her for a long, thoughtful moment. "Rune. You know what that's like."

She flushed. "Yeah."

He pulled her into the kitchen. All her men, except for Owen, were gathered around the table, eating as though there would be no more food.

"Lex okay?" she asked.

Levi took a swallow of coffee and nodded. "She wants to see you before you go in."

Rune piled a plate with eggs and bacon, grabbed a cup of coffee, and went to Lex's bedroom. She hadn't had a chance to update the Other and it was past time she did.

"Can you eat a little?" she asked Lex, when she walked into the bedroom.

Lex lay with a stack of pillows behind her, watching music videos. "Ellie brought me broth earlier. I kept it down. I don't want to chance eggs." She shuddered.

"How are you feeling?"

"Awful." She hesitated. "Can you…smell me?"

"No, baby," Rune lied.

She left the plate of food on the bureau and carried her coffee to the bed. She sat down carefully, studying Lex's face.

The girl's cheekbones stood out in sharp relief, making her sluggish, feverish eyes appear even more sunken than they already were. Her skin was splitting in places, and her lips looked like overly ripe slices of fruit that were about to burst and spew their contents upon her chin.

Strangely enough, she was more lucid than she'd been in the Annex clinic.

"You've been through so much fucking sickness, Lex. You'll get through this one, too. Then maybe you should start taking some vitamins."

Lex managed a quick grin. "Maybe."

"I'm going to Skyll. As soon as I can."

"And I'll go with you. The cure is there."

"Yes."

"Denim told me the crew can't go with us."

"He's right. It's not possible."

"Then we'll have to come back."

"We will." She paused. "Both of us."

Lex didn't ask her what she meant. Likely, she already knew.

Rune started to take a sip of her coffee when her cell rang. "Elizabeth," Rune said. "Everything okay?"

"Rune."

Rune stood quickly, frowning. "Fie? What's wrong?"

Fie breathed into the phone. "Bad men came," she said, finally.

Gooseflesh erupted on Rune's skin, and she pushed a fist into her stake scars. "I'm on my way, honey. I'm going to put Ellis on the phone—you remember Ellis? He'll talk to you until I get there."

"Rune," Lex called, as Rune started to leave the room. "What happened?"

"Elizabeth's in trouble." Rune ran to the kitchen. Her men jumped to their feet as soon as they saw the look on her face. "One of you call Eugene. Get to Elizabeth's house as soon as you can." She tossed Ellis her phone.

"Keep Fie calm until I get there."

And without another word, she was out the door. She didn't even think of taking her car. Her monster was faster than a car.

The front of Elizabeth's house was surrounded by a fence of hedges. Rune knew at least one guard, probably two, had been placed somewhere near the front. The back, enclosed by a privacy fence, would have contained more ops, and at least two of them had been stationed inside.

There was no sign of any of them.

When she was at the front door, she stood there for five impossible seconds, terrified of what she'd discover inside.

Her heart hurt her chest.

"Shit," she cried, and shoved open the unlocked door.

The entryway was empty.

But she smelled the blood.

"Elizabeth," she yelled. She found the first dead operative lying with a broken neck outside the living room. The scent of blood was not coming from him.

Inside the living room was…

Horror.

Just horror.

And blood, there was that.

Fie squatted beside Elizabeth, the cell phone on the floor.

For an instant, Rune was the one crouched on a floor slick with blood, the dead lying around her.

She shook her head once, hard, and walked carefully to Fie, stepping over cut and bloody bodies. She slipped as her boot skidded through blood.

The room was a scene of destruction and death. She counted the bodies of fourteen more ops. Fifteen, she realized, when she spotted one of them up against the fireplace.

She knelt down beside Fie and Elizabeth. "Elizabeth," she whispered.

But Elizabeth was long dead. Her throat had been cut.

Rune looked at Fie. "What happened?"

Fie, her skeletal little face somber, looked away from Elizabeth. "The bad men came."

Rune nodded. "Can you tell me what happened then?"

"They made her bleed," Fie said. "They hurt her. She fell down."

"Okay, baby."

"The guards got killed too."

Rune's swallow hurt her throat. She heard cars roaring up the street and knew her men had arrived.

Not all of the dead were Annex ops. Some of the dead were Fie's "bad men."

"Who killed the bad men, honey?"

Fie's barely there lips lifted in a proud smile and the innocent ice in her eyes chilled Rune's heart.

"I did," the child said, shrugging. "But I didn't kill Owen. I let him go, 'cause I like Owen."

CHAPTER THIRTY-TWO

Rune heard someone behind her before Fie jumped to her feet, squealing. "Uncle B'serk!"

She closed her eyes, unable to turn and look at him.

She knew what she'd see when she did.

Owen, how the fuck could you?

"Fie," she said, keeping her stare on Elizabeth's body, "was Owen one of the bad men?"

"I like Owen," Fie said.

Rune climbed to her feet, her pants soaked through with blood, and walked to where Strad held the little necromancer. "Did he kill Elizabeth?"

Fie hid her face against the berserker's neck. "He made me not look."

Fuck. Rune shuddered, and finally, she looked at the berserker.

He met her stare calmly, his eyes filled with worry. Pain. Pity.

"I'm sorry, sweetheart," he told her.

"Why would he do this?" she murmured. "Why?

Don't trust Owen Five.

But she *had* trusted him, just a little fucking bit.

"We'll ask him when we find him," he replied, handing Fie to Denim. And then, he let his rage peek out at her. But only for a second.

"What the fuck went on here?" Jack asked, striding into

the room. He stopped when he spotted Elizabeth's body. "Shit. Son of a bitch." And then he whispered, so low no one could hear him, *"Mom."*

But Rune heard and her heart broke for him. Bill and Elizabeth had become sort of a stand-in mom and dad to the crew.

"Owen's work," Strad growled.

Jack shook his head. "No. He wouldn't have done this."

"There has to be a reason," Rune said. "Something…"

"It doesn't matter if he had a hundred reasons. He's a dead man," the berserker said.

The cowboy had left them no choice. She could no longer defend him.

Owen had betrayed them all.

He'd betrayed her.

But at the back of her mind was a tiny, insistent voice, telling her that maybe, maybe…

Maybe there was a good reason. Maybe he wasn't a traitor.

Maybe he hadn't killed Elizabeth.

She had to find out.

She didn't want to say the words aloud, not right then, with the crew confused and angry and hurt. Not with Strad glaring around the room with death in his stare.

She did anyway. "Before we kill him, we're going to give him a chance to explain. We're going to give him the benefit of the doubt and not judge him as guilty until we know for sure."

Her voice was hard, but her stomach rolled so violently she was sure she'd throw up if she opened her mouth again.

Owen.

Fuck you.

Bill flung himself into the room, his eyes wild. "Oh, no. Oh, not Elizabeth."

Then, he saw her.

He went to her, slowly, and dropped to his knees. He picked up her hand. "She's gone, then. Really gone."

Annex ops came into the house, guns drawn.

"Put those away," Rune snapped. "You're a little too fucking late." She pressed her palms into her eyes and tried to breathe through the pain. Elizabeth was dead. Dead.

And Owen…

"What happened?" Bill turned his tortured eyes to Rune. "My God, Rune. What happened?"

"Some bad men," Rune murmured.

"Pardon?"

"Fie said some bad men came in and killed Elizabeth." Rune looked at Fie, frowning, suddenly remembering what Fie had said. "She said she killed them."

"Elizabeth did?"

"No. Fie did." Rune motioned at Denim. "Take her to…"

Take her where? The Annex, to Eugene, so he could put her in a sterile cage and study her for the rest of her life?

"Take her to Ellis," Strad said. "We'll figure it out later."

Rune nodded, relieved. "Yes. To Ellis."

Denim headed out the door with the unprotesting child.

Rune stood beside Bill and put a hand on his shoulder. "The men killed our ops," she told him. "They killed Elizabeth. From what I can understand, Fie killed the men. I don't know how. I didn't know she could…"

She shrugged and continued. "Fie killed the ones she called the bad men, except for one."

He looked up at her, a spark of interest cutting through his grief. "Who?"

Rune opened her mouth, but nothing came out. She couldn't say his name.

Strad had no such problem. "Owen."

"No," Bill said. "Owen loved Elizabeth. They were

close."

"Yeah," Rune said. "Maybe not so much."

Bill's cell rang but he ignored it.

Rune's began ringing as soon as his stopped, and she felt a deep stab of pain when she realized Elizabeth would never call her again.

"It's Eugene," she said. "I don't want to talk to fucking Eugene."

Raze took her cell. "I'll do it."

He stomped from the room, his deep voice rumbling, the cell to his ear.

Strad's gaze went with an almost weary hesitancy to the splashes of blood coloring the floor. He glanced at Elizabeth's cold, sad body, at Bill, hunched and devastated, and then, he looked at Rune.

"Strad," she said. "Wait."

But he turned and strode from the room, beginning a search for Owen Five that wouldn't end until one of them was dead.

CHAPTER THIRTY-THREE

"Why would they kill Elizabeth?" Levi asked, as he drove Rune to Wormwood.

"I think they were after Fie. She…" She stared out the window, unsure. What the hell was the child?

"Yeah," he said. "The net didn't just change her physically, did it?"

"I don't know what it did to her." But the girl was as deadly as anyone Rune had ever met.

They'd examined the bodies before they'd handed the horrific crime scene and Elizabeth over to the Annex housekeeping. The corpses were covered with blood, but it was as though it'd exploded from their pores. There were no wounds.

The wounds were on the Annex operatives. Their attempts at defense had been shut down quickly and quietly. They'd been stabbed, and some of them had broken necks.

No one had been shot.

Eugene told Raze it might have been the Next, but he wasn't sure. He wasn't sure about anything.

None of them were.

After all, they'd thought the Next was responsible for the rotting sickness.

"And Owen," Levi said. "That was some bad shit back there."

"But you don't think he did it."

He shook his head, and his long braid slid over his shoulder. "I don't know. He was there. Fie couldn't make that up. But *why* was he there?"

"Fie said he made her turn away when Elizabeth was killed." Rune put a hand to her throat, her breath hitching. Dammit. She would have to mourn Elizabeth.

She'd hide from it for as long as she could.

She punched her leg, suddenly, then winced at the pain. The disease was making her weaker. "Owen is not the enemy. Owen is not the bad guy. He's *not,* Levi. Oh, fuck." She crossed her arms over her midsection and leaned forward, glad Levi was driving. "*Is* he?"

Levi patted her shoulder. "Maybe, Rune."

When they arrived at Wormwood, Strad's car was already there.

"You called it," Levi said.

"I knew he'd search Wormwood first."

The huge graveyard was a perfect place to hide. It was huge.

But if Owen was inside the gates, Gunnar would know it.

He wouldn't help Strad find Owen—but he'd help her.

Owen *was* there. Bill had him tracked through his cell phone. Strad wasn't the only man who wanted a piece of the cowboy.

She wanted to get to Owen before the berserker did. She wanted answers.

Strad just wanted to kill him.

She and Levi stepped into the graveyard, and Gunnar was waiting.

He didn't speak or wait for her to speak, just turned and ran.

She and Levi were right behind him.

Gunnar slowed when he reached a copse of trees—the very trees that he'd once been buried beneath, in a box too small for his long body.

He turned to look at her then, and with his dark stare pinned upon her, he pointed. "There are your men, Your Highness."

She'd underestimated Strad. Or maybe, Owen had never meant to hide when he'd gone to the graveyard.

It didn't matter. Not then.

What mattered was that the cowboy and the berserker were facing off, and Rune wasn't ready to let either one of them die.

Too many people were dying.

She was suddenly, inexplicably furious.

"I have questions," she screamed, breaking the skin of her palms with her nails.

She was aware that she looked and sounded like a mad woman, and she didn't care at all. She streaked into the clearing, screaming. Raging.

She was hurting.

And that made her want to hurt them.

They both snapped their heads around to look at her, their eyes a little wide, concerned, and familiar.

Oh God, I do love them. I love them. I love them.

That helped her go quiet, just a little.

"Bastards," she said, breathing hard, understanding in that moment how easy it would be for her to snap and kill them both.

Shhhh. Shhhh…

Her monster rubbed against her insides, purring, eager to get out. Eager to kill.

But she wouldn't let it kill them—she was there to save them.

Her mind was overwhelmed, and her heart had broken too many times. That made her a very dangerous monster, even to the ones she loved.

Because they were pissing her the fuck off.

She felt Levi at her back. Gunnar was there somewhere, as well, probably peering around a tree.

And I'm here, sweet thing.

She nodded.

Finally, she looked at the two men.

She pointed at Owen. "Explain, if you want to live."

Her voice was like gravel, hard and bumpy and covering secret dark things that had gotten stomped below the rock.

"No," Strad said, his own rage boiling over. "I'm killing him. Levi, take her the fuck out of here."

As if.

As if anyone could take her somewhere she did not want to go.

She glanced at Levi.

He held up his palms and backed away.

She shuddered with the effort it took her to remain composed. "I will hear his story. There are things we need to know. Let him explain."

"He's full of lies, Rune," the berserker roared. "He will tell us no part of the truth."

"Owen," she said. Begged.

"I..." But then, he shook his head. He'd lost his hat. He watched her, something in his eyes she couldn't decipher. But for one brief second, pain flared. Then there was nothing on his face but resignation. "I've got no excuses."

She took a staggering step back, stunned.

"Nothing?" Levi said, baffled. "Owen?"

Owen shrugged. "I'm so sorry. But I couldn't—"

The berserker hit him, his fist crumbling Owen's face like a sledge hammer on plaster.

Rune couldn't move, couldn't process that Owen was unable and unwilling to vindicate himself.

To give them something.

He was fucking *crew*.

She'd clung to hope, but hope had kicked her away and flung her into the darkness.

And nothing made sense.

For a long, long minute of agonizing confusion, she

was unable to move.

Strad was gone, lost in his own world of madness and rage.

She was a child, suddenly. Muddled and hurt and helpless. "I'm rotting." She held up her hands and looked at them, then showed them to men who were not watching. "See? I'm *rotting*."

Levi grabbed her wrists. "Rune. *Rune.*"

And she came back.

Strad dragged Owen from the ground, Owen, who was somehow still alive, and began to beat him with a rage that no one could have forced him to contain.

Not even Rune.

But she would try.

"Berserker," she yelled, and ran to him.

Her legs were shaking, and her mind was full of chaos and noise.

So she listened to her heart.

"Rune," Owen said, barely understandable as he managed to speak through swollen, torn lips. "You know me."

She grabbed Strad's huge arm. "You can't hurt him like that," she whispered. "You can't do that."

He looked at her, but there was only rage in his eyes.

"Okay," he murmured, surprising her.

For one second, her heart jumped with gladness. With relief.

Then the berserker yanked his arm free from her grip, pulled his gun, and shot Owen in the chest.

The cowboy dropped like a stone, his hand to his wound. He didn't make a sound.

"Ah," Rune said. "No."

As she stared, shocked and disbelieving, Owen climbed somehow to his feet. Bent forward at the waist, his hand to his chest, he staggered away.

Strad grabbed her arm, hard, as she started after the cowboy. "No. Let him go. Once and for all, Rune, let him fucking go."

"I can't." Her voice was shaking, but calm. Deadly, horribly calm. "I won't let any of my crew wander off to die alone."

And though he held her in a grip too powerful for any human to break, not even the berserker was strong enough to hold her monster.

CHAPTER THIRTY-FOUR

She was too late.

She flew through Wormwood like a monster possessed, but not as fast as she could have for fear of running right past his hiding place and his shot, damaged body.

Owen was gone.

Blood remained, droplets of Owen's life that had drained from his body, decorating the hard earth.

She was too late.

He was gone.

She knew he was gone because the infinitesimal spark that was Owen wasn't there anymore, and the world was changed.

The cowboy was dead.

She felt the absence of him.

She stumbled as her tears blinded her. Life was impossible and she had so much more of it to get through. An eternity of losing people. A forever of pain.

She'd lost Gunnar, the berserker, Elizabeth, Owen…

Gunnar and Strad had come back to her.

Elizabeth and Owen would not.

She even mourned the vampire master and his colorful sidekick. She grieved for the death of River County Others.

For her city.

Lex was dying.

Fie was a monster.

Rune was rotting.

She fell to her knees and let her head hang, too tired to keep going.

The rotting disease was getting stronger by the minute, and she was getting weaker. She could feel it streaming through her body, blackening her insides, pulping her organs.

Wearying her brain, her thoughts, her spirit.

She wanted to scream in rage but all that came out when she opened her mouth was a wail of anguish.

She didn't like change. She didn't like death.

And she had no control over either of those things.

At last, she got to her feet and started back through Wormwood.

There was nothing else to do.

Owen was dead.

Dead like Z.

Levi was waiting for her, but the berserker had gone.

"He said he knew you'd want some time," Levi told her.

"Yeah," she said. "Time."

Jack and Raze waited by the gates, and she caught herself looking automatically for Owen before she remembered.

"What exactly happened?" Jack asked Levi, as they exited the graveyard.

"Strad beat Owen nearly to death. Then he shot him." Levi's voice was grim, but still a little disbelieving.

"Owen's dead?" Raze asked. "Strad killed him?"

Levi looked at Rune.

"I couldn't find him. He's..." she shrugged, and forced back tired tears. "He's gone. He was shot in the chest. He won't live through that."

"How did he get away?" Jack asked. "Beaten and shot, how did he get away?"

"I don't know how one human could take so much

damage," Levi said. "Remember the first time Strad beat the fuck out of him?"

"Maybe he's not human," Raze said, not looking at any of them.

"He's human." Rune pushed her hair out of her face. "Just some kind of super human."

"Rune." Jack frowned. "How sick *are* you?"

So they knew. It wasn't just Ellie fearing the worst.

"Pretty fucking sick," she admitted. "But I can go a lot longer than Lex can. She's the one we need to worry about."

"Is Owen really dead?" Levi asked.

They kept jumping back and forth between subjects, but Rune knew it was because each issue was too heavy not to put away for a few seconds and concentrate on something else.

No one answered him, but they had no doubt that soon, the cowboy's body would be found half-hidden in some hollow he'd dug into the side of a hill, or camouflaged beneath the thickness of some brambles and vines.

Or gnawed on by a starving, rotting Other.

Rune shuddered.

"Owen and Elizabeth, both on the same day. That's fucked up." Jack adjusted his eye patch. "That's real fu—"

"Rune."

Rune jerked her head around at the soft voice interrupting Jack. "What the hell?"

The crew rushed back to the gates and then inside, where Fie stood, with her feet bare and her hair still damp from the careful washing Ellie must have given it.

"Fie," Rune said, shrugging off her coat to drape around the child. "How did you get here? Where's Ellis?"

"I'm going outside the gates to call Denim," Levi said, as he hurried away.

Jack yanked the child off the cold ground and held her against his chest as they waited for Fie to answer.

"I walked." She squirmed impatiently. "Let me down. I have to go with Rune."

Rune opened her arms. "Give her to me."

Jack transferred the little necromancer to Rune.

"I'll take you home, baby," Rune told her, but fear left a bad taste in her mouth. The only way Fie could have gotten away from Ellie and Denim was if something had happened to them.

Please God, no more.

"Raze," she murmured.

He nodded and strode away to find out from Levi what the hell had happened.

Jack squeezed her arm. "They're okay. This kid is a slippery little thing."

"No," Fie cried, when Rune began to carry her back toward the gates. "We can't go."

And Rune got an even worse feeling.

She had to try twice before she could get the words out. "Why not, Fie?"

"You know why not." Fie's dark eyes, distended and grotesque in her skeletal face, held something too old and too terrifying for a tiny girl.

A lack, somehow, of humanity.

Just a cold impatience.

"Fie?" Rune whispered. "Why not?"

Fie sighed. "It's time. The bells are ringing."

Rune shivered. "I don't hear bells."

"I do," Fie said. "I hear bells. You hear…"

"Echoes," Rune finished.

"Do you hear the echoes, Rune?" Jack's face had paled, and his voice rose in alarm.

"I can't go by myself," Fie said, calm. "You have to take me."

"Do you *hear* them, Rune?" Jack was sliding quickly into full out panic mode.

So was Rune. "I can't go yet," she told Fie. "We have to get Lex."

"No," Fie said, then more loudly, when Rune started hurrying with her toward the gates. "No!"

Gunnar stepped out in front of her. "Rune. Stop."

"I can't, Gunnar." She was almost unable to get the words out. "I have to get Lex."

Jack grabbed her arm to drag her on. "Out of the way, ghoul."

Fie struggled harder and began to cry. "No." And finally, she sounded like the child she was. "I want to *go.*"

"God," Rune yelled.

Levi and Raze ran back into the graveyard.

"What is it?" Raze roared, his blades in his hands.

Levi looked around, trying to find the threat.

No one was there but Gunnar.

"The echoes," Rune managed to gasp out. Oh, she heard them. She smelled them. She felt them.

How did I forget?
I'm here, sweet thing.
Rune, you know me.
It's time.

Fie wrapped her arms around Rune's neck and held on as tightly as she could, weeping.

Rune's entire body shook with tremors too strong to stop. Her brain froze. Her voice left her.

I know you.
How did I forget?
Lex, she screamed, silently. *Lex.*

But Lex was sick and her demon, at that moment, was dead.

Rune couldn't call it.

Lex would die if Rune left her.

She ground her teeth, moaning, shaking.

"Your Highness," Gunnar cried, or she thought he did.

His thin hands were crossed over his chest, his mouth opening and closing as he sobbed.

Her mind swirled, swirled with a cacophony of voices and memories and dark wind. Echoes. Terrible, terrifying echoes.

He's ours now.
Blood and Fire.
Blood and Fire.
Bloo—

And then they surrounded her, the huge animals, and she wanted to cry from happiness and cry from fear.

Sadness.

Insanity.

The berserker was there, suddenly, finally, horribly, his face crumbling, his eyes agonized, roaring, calling, pleading.

He reached for her.

He grabbed air.

Because Rune was gone.

The echoes had taken her.

CHAPTER THIRTY-FIVE

Fire ate her.

Ate her, boiled her flesh away, left clean, white bone, and finally, spit her out on the other side.

But before the fire there was ice, and images, and a path marked by skulls and tortured, reaching hands and begging souls.

Before the fire there was darkness and silence and nothingness so complete she knew she was dead.

And wind.

Wind that held every voice that ever was, every life that ever formed.

There were screams so bone-chilling she almost, at first, didn't feel the fire.

But the fire. Oh, God.

The fire.

There would never be words to describe the fire. To explain how it consumed her. How it changed her.

Blood and Fire didn't protect her from that—they couldn't. They could only guide her, the spirit dogs, to where she needed to go.

When she was spewed out into the world of Skyll, her first thought was of Gunnar.

Gunnar the Ghoul, who'd traipsed that very path, that very horrifying and agonizing path, for her.

She lay upon the alien but strangely familiar ground,

and was unable to move.

She remained clothed but felt as though the garments had forged themselves into her skin. She was too weak to feel for her weapons.

Fie cried, somewhere in the distance, but Rune couldn't comfort the child. She lay stunned and disassembled, broken and shattered.

She was frozen, and she was scorched.

And images, teasing and not quite there, like forgotten words on the tip of her tongue.

What had she seen?

Something. Something important.

But the images had floated away.

She didn't care.

Maybe five minutes later, or five years later, she opened her mouth, amazed that she could do so. "Fie," she said, her voice cracking.

She had to get the crying to stop.

She slid her hand across the hard, dusty ground and sharp rocks scratched eagerly at her palm—it felt good. Anything would have felt good after the agony she'd just endured.

At last, she dragged herself to a sitting position and lifted her hands to shove her hair out of her face.

She was moving, feeling, alive.

Stronger.

And she got her first look at Skyll.

Barren, charred earth stretched out before her, brown and red and bleached white.

The sky was so blue it hurt her to look at it.

She could smell everything—water and heat and plants and animals. Smoke, meat, air polluted by chemicals. Exhaust and shit and sweat.

And Fie continued to cry, long, plaintive cries that had no end.

Rune put her hands over her ears, but it did no good. The crying went on and on and on…

She stood. Somehow, she stood.

She felt, for at least two minutes, as though she were looking through a tunnel. And she couldn't see Fie anywhere.

The cries had no direction.

Slowly, her vision cleared.

The dogs were gone.

Fie was gone.

She was alone.

"Oh," she said. There was no crying. Not really. Just inside her head.

And when she acknowledged it, the crying stopped.

She stood on a small, rocky hill. In front of her was desert, but when she turned, she was happy to see trees. A cool, serene forest.

She shaded her eyes. "Fie," she yelled. Her voice was rusty and harsh, but it was loud. "Fie!"

Fie wasn't there. She could only hope Blood and Fire had carried the child to safety. She felt little fear for the necromancer. She knew, as well as Fie had, that the little girl belonged in Skyll.

Whatever part of Skyll she'd landed in appeared unoccupied. There were no birds singing, no small animals darting, no—

An unfamiliar noise behind her broke the silence and she spun, crouching. She shot out her claws, not realizing until that second how afraid she'd been that her monster would not come.

It came, bringing claws and fangs and speed. She didn't feel as sick, but the rotting disease continued to flow through her like a brown, polluted river.

Probably its progress would be slowed because that world was created of magic, just as she was. Whatever the reason, she felt a little less sick.

Maybe that would give her more time. More time to deal with the horrors sure to come. More time to find the cure.

It would not, however, give Lex more time. Or any of the Others.

Her monster had not deserted her, and if there was any little spark of light to cling to, it was that.

But the thing in front of her...

She gasped and stumbled backward, her brain unable to comprehend what her eyes were seeing.

It did not belong in that world of magic and silence and heat.

It was a huge, mechanical, man-shaped piece of equipment, rusty in parts and shiny in others. Its head squeaked as it turned it to survey her.

It may have been there all along, but her mind had been delayed from the trip over and had taken its time catching up with her body.

A sudden black cloud appeared in the distant burning sky, and it was only when she began to hear the raucous cries that she understood the black cloud was actually a huge formation of crows.

A murder of crows.

Their calls were strident and mocking, and as she watched, they dive-bombed the metal apparition.

All she could do was stand and gape.

The thing opened its jaws, and a sound like twisting metal emerged. Loud and excruciating.

She put her hands over her ears again and backed away, then turned and ran for the woods.

How did one fight a machine as tall as the trees and made up of metal? There was nothing to do but run. And hide.

The machine did not follow.

Neither did the crows.

She stumbled farther into the woods, and when she was sure the thing wasn't coming, she stopped to take stock of her body and her belongings.

One of her ammunition belts flapped, broken and ragged and empty, and she tossed it to the ground. Her clothes were tattered, but clung to her body stubbornly. One of her blades had dropped into her left boot, and she caressed the sharp silver for a second before sliding it into a remaining sheath.

She tied her boots. One of the strings broke when she pulled it and she cursed, as though a broken bootlace really mattered.

There was nothing else, but she didn't need her weapons. She had her monster.

And she appreciated the hell out of it.

She pushed sweat-drenched strands of hair out of her face and continued on, slowly. The forest was watching her, its breath held.

She could feel it like a heavy weight across her back.

Paths, long and white, stretched out before her, twisting between trees until they were out of sight. The light from the bright sun had trouble penetrating more deeply into the woods, and she was hesitant as she wandered farther into the gloom.

But she went on, more comfortable with the woods than the scorching sun and the…metal man.

There had to be people somewhere—Gunnar had assured her of that. There would be towns. Cities.

Allies.

She just had to find them.

Shivers overtook her as the reality of her situation began to sink in.

A sudden screech sounded, reverberating through the woods. She ducked behind a tree and peered around it grimly, shuddering like a little girl watching a horror movie.

And when she realized that fact, she straightened her spine.

She was Rune Alexander.

She wasn't going to cower behind a tree in *any* world.

Not even if that world belonged to Damascus.

She strode back to the path, her fists clenched. "Fuck you," she screamed.

The screech came again, closer, and she saw movement high in the treetops.

"Fucking bird," she muttered.

She hoped.

She walked on.

As she walked, the woods woke up—creatures began to scurry, leaves began to wave, and finally, birds began to sing.

Still, the woods were eerie.

Strange.

She picked a path and stuck with it, following it faithfully.

And when the screech came again, she shot out her claws. She could handle anything that bled.

She wished *something* would show itself, because she'd rather fight than face nothing.

But she was not to fight in the forest that day.

The path ended, the trees parted, and she stepped out into the world of her nightmares.

CHAPTER THIRTY-SIX

The other side of the woods was dark.

Nighttime.

The sun no longer baked the world with blistering heat. The moon, a cold, silver sickle, ruled the sky.

Fire and explosions lit up the darkness, the blasts miles away, and she stared down on thousands of tiny, yellow lights.

A city.

Something huge and even darker than the sky streaked through the air above, releasing golden flames with a roaring rush she could almost feel.

Not a plane, though.

A demon.

Air from its flapping, swooshing wings fanned her cheeks with a hot wind that smelled of wood smoke. It was the scent of Lex's breath after she'd had her Damascus-induced seizure.

She wanted to fall to ground and hide her face. To sleep and wake up in the berserker's arms. To see her crew.

But she started down the hill.

Not slowly. With her claws out and ready, she ran, taking horror and death to a city that seemed to already have more than its share.

She became…herself.

The trip had stripped more than her weapons from her—it'd stripped something inside her that made her Rune Alexander.

Stripped something that made her remember she was immortal, and even had she not been, she was not afraid to die.

And at that moment, she took it the fuck back.

She ran, elation deep and dark inside her as she streaked through the night, hoping an innocent didn't suddenly appear in her path—she'd have killed it.

She was death.

There was no other way to be. Not there.

You were born of blood and magic.
And you were born of death.

The words came sliding into her mind, then crept teasingly into a corner to crouch quietly until she was ready to examine them.

At that moment, she was home.

When she embraced it, when she accepted it, she felt the world open its arms.

It had been waiting for her.

There were so many sounds. So many sights.

The dark sky was constantly brightened by explosions as colorful and quick as fireworks. Screams began to trickle to her ears the closer she drew to the city.

Other instruments played in that horror of an orchestra—unfamiliar and grating and out of sync. Roars that came from no human, groans that split the night, high-pitched shrieks that could have shattered glass.

Before she reached the city she began to see shapes streaking across the ground—wolves, yes, wolves—and shadows that were as flat and insubstantial and fleeting as spirits.

Vampires.

Oh, God, vampires.

Hers.

She screamed with joy.

Fighting and killing she understood.

An ephemeral hand, fingers like long, purple smears, appeared in the sky. She was near enough to the city to hear screams of terror and the occasional shout of, "the hand, the hand!" before the fingers disappeared.

She had no idea what retribution the hand had brought or would bring, but she was sure it was harsh.

Harsh, horrible magic.

She climbed the huge stone wall surrounding the city, the useless wall that couldn't keep magic or fire or bombs out, and it couldn't keep Rune Alexander out.

She crouched for a second atop it, surveying the pandemonium below.

Tall streetlights and moving spotlights lit the area, along with the moon and the near constant explosions, fires, and flame-breathing creatures.

People ran, animals scampered, and fighters armed with bows and arrows, blades, axes, and blowguns fought like people possessed.

When she stood and prepared to leap into the noisy crowds below, she saw more people rushing through a crumbled section of stone wall.

The city had been infiltrated and was under attack. It was being destroyed.

An image of River County flashed into her mind, and a stab of homesickness hit her so hard she bent double, trying to breathe through the pain.

For that world, too, was her home.

She grabbed onto her thirst for blood. Once again in control, she held up her claws and leaped into the chaos.

She couldn't differentiate the bad guys from the good guys—if it came at her, she killed it.

Slicing through shifters, vampires, and other creatures she was unfamiliar with. Men, women…

Others.

They were *all* Others.

She fought her way through the city, ducking into

alleyways exactly like the ones back home, smashing through shop windows, chasing down beings that appeared to be foul-smelling trolls.

Strange creatures that resembled mountainous men with bodies of enormous dogs streaked by her. They were ridden by men.

And she realized she'd chosen a side, even though she hadn't been aware of it.

It became obvious that the interlopers, the city destroyers, were not the vampires or shifters or wolves. They were not the men and women valiantly and skillfully wielding sharp silver and deadly arrows.

The interlopers were the strange creatures she didn't recognize—and the men who rode them.

Those men carried whips. Whips of fire, magic, and poison. She saw victims of the whips fall, froth spilling from their mouths, eyes rolling back into their heads.

She saw the whips carve out sections of brick buildings and create craters in the pavement upon which they landed.

The whips cut bodies in half, neatly and quickly.

One of the creatures grabbed a man who brandished a sword nearly as long as he was tall and batted away the blade.

Even as he galloped through the crowds, he held his victim beneath him, thrusting, grunting like a thousand pigs. He raped the man as the man who rode *him* continued to sling his whip against the fighters of the city.

She went after the intruders, rage boiling inside her.

They were, surely, that world's COS.

She chose a side.

And gradually, those she fought with began to notice her.

As did their enemies.

Three fighters—a man and two women—paused to watch her for a second before running to fight beside her.

There was no time to talk.

Much.

"Nice," the man said. "Those are some claws, lady."

She pulled her claws free of a charging beast's belly and grinned.

Then she noticed that her claws, which had faded to muted silver in her world, had grown brighter. The longer she fought, the brighter they became until finally, they radiated a shining silver too bright to stare at for long.

And that drew a lot of attention.

People began to move closer to her, fighting with her as though they accepted her as one of them.

And those people were hardcore.

She'd thought she'd witnessed every atrocity possible, but she'd been wrong.

Shiv Crew fought hard, but there was always a sort of humanity to their fighting. They killed, but always protected. They'd have done anything to protect each other.

The ones she fought with and against in Skyll were...monsters. She felt it. Maybe they knew nothing else.

Or maybe they knew something she didn't.

But damned if they didn't shock the hell out of her.

"Tiff," one of the men beside her shouted, and as Rune turned at his voice, she watched him shove his sword through the girl who fought with him just so he could pin the enemy who was trying to kill her.

He hadn't hesitated or tried to find a way to save her and kill the enemy. Just killed them both and then went back to fighting.

And slowly, the city began to push the attackers out.

The moon was red. When she caught a glimpse of it through the haze of blood that misted the air, it was red.

She shivered.

One of the beasts galloped by Rune, his rider unfurling his whip to fling at a red-haired girl with a slingshot. A fucking slingshot.

Rune growled, but before she could jump on top of the beast and send the whip-wielder to hell, the girl turned, grinned, and shot the beast between its eyes.

It fell.

Not slowly, not gradually, but immediately.

Just dropped like a boulder and didn't move again.

"Showing off, Roma?" a man yelled, his voice full of laughter.

The sudden stop propelled the rider off its back and sent him tumbling violently toward the girl.

Rune caught him with her claws, decapitating him as he flew through the air.

The girl met Rune's stare for a moment, then shrugged and went back to the fight.

Rune shook her head as she fought. A fucking *slingshot*.

But the girl was good with it. And fast.

Shiv Crew material.

She shook off the pain that screamed through her when she thought of her crew and lost herself in the battle.

A battle that would soon be over.

The enemy was retreating. Slowly, but they were retreating.

Those that refused to withdraw were dying.

The blood ran freely, thick and hot, and she didn't pause to consider what feasting in Skyll might mean. She drank.

She needed to feed—it was as simple as that.

At least, it was that simple to her.

She sliced open one of the beast's throats, ran her claws through his master's chest, then fell to her knees to drink of the blood spurting from the ugly, dying beast.

The blood spread through her veins like cold water, and she frowned. He wasn't a tasty enemy. As a matter of fact, he tasted of...

Damascus.

"Fuck me," she said. "That sucks."

People were staring at her.

They stopped fighting to watch her.

Some with doubt, some with horror, some with interest.

All of them with fear.

And awe.

Word spread like a terrible disease, swiftly and surely, touching everyone who stood there.

Every one of them reacted to that one feeding.

The enemy turned and fled.

The ones whose city she'd defended fell to their knees before her.

They held their fists to their chests, over their hearts.

They knelt on the ground, bleeding and wounded and agonized, but their eyes were shining.

She couldn't at first make out what they'd begun to mutter, until they lifted their voices in unison, joyful and strong.

"Our princess," they shouted, "has come."

CHAPTER THIRTY-SEVEN

She shook her head and backed away, her hands up. "No."

"Your Highness." Their whispered words undulated through the crowd like a breeze through a field of wheat.

Your Highness…

She closed her eyes in a long, slow blink.

From above, one of the fire-breathing creatures that had set the trees and homes of the city ablaze screeched and dive-bombed the crowd.

"He's out of fire," one of them yelled, but they jumped to their feet and scattered, moving out of the beast's way.

The slingshot girl, Roma, scrambled backward and took aim at the falling creature with her insignificant-looking weapon, and Rune took advantage of the citizens' sudden lack of attention and ran.

She was vampire, magic, whatever the fuck—

And she could *run*.

She was gone in seconds.

Your Highness.

She shuddered as she ran through the crumbling, destroyed city, her heart hurting, her brain ready to explode.

Your Highness.

Our princess has come.

She started moaning and couldn't quit.

And she ran.

It was too much. Everything was too much.

An insidious knowledge, secretive and slimy and ancient, grew like a cancer in her brain. In her memory.

Torturing her.

Confusing her.

Your Highness.

Once she left the city behind she stopped running, staggered into a tree, and vomited up the blood she'd ingested.

It burned like fire.

And she was fucking alone.

Fuck you, Gunnar.

I know you.

How did I forget?

"Oh," Rune cried. "Oh God!"

She beat the hard bark until the tree disintegrated and her fists were a pulpy, bloody mess.

And finally, she wiped her nose on the tail of her shirt and turned to survey a dark world that was not her own.

Was *not*.

"I need to go home," she murmured.

Somewhere off in the distance a colossal blast shook the ground and lit up the sky. She didn't move, already accustomed to the explosions of the new place, but the boom flushed a few dozen animals—not wolves, nor shifters, nor the beasts the whip men had ridden—from some hiding place near her.

They streaked by, huffing and yelping, their huge paws tearing up the hard earth as they went.

Mutations.

Big as horses and ugly as…

Monsters.

Huge, hairy monsters with unimaginable faces and brown teeth as long and sharp as vampire stakes. They excreted feces as they ran—steaming piles of foulness that made her cover her nose and gag.

Gone in a flash.

It was a world not of Others, but of monsters.

Monsters like her.

"Girlie…"

She spun around, her claws already out, fangs dropping.

No one was there.

"Girlie…"

"Show yourself," she demanded.

"I hear your heart beating. Fast…so fast. Your fear is delightful."

"Fuck you," she said. "*I'm* not the one hiding."

She turned in slow circles, trying to catch a glimpse of the one who taunted her. The voice was low and whispery, and she had no idea if the owner of that voice was male or female.

"Oh girlie. You don't want me to show myself. You would faint, and I would feast upon your lovely flesh. *All* of it."

Rune forced her claws to lengthen. She smacked them together like silver knives then held them out and ready at her sides. "I'm not the fainting type. Come on. Take a chance."

Then another voice, quiet and terse but so thick she could barely understand the words, came from the shadows. "Back off, Celia."

"But I want it," Celia said. "Oh, so badly."

"Go."

"Well?" Rune asked him, once Celia's angry footsteps had faded. "Who the fuck are *you?*"

But she backed away. She really didn't care who anyone was. She just needed to find Damascus, get a cure—though she was beginning to doubt that'd be possible—and get back to her crew.

To the dying Others of her world.

To *Lex*.

If she could find a way back.

The man said nothing. He'd slunk away, back into the shadows of the forest, following the faceless Celia.

Once again, she was alone.

Or as alone as she could be, with the hidden creatures and monsters of Skyll lurking under every rock and behind every tree.

But she caught a scent as she walked away, a light, teasing scent.

She stopped walking, uncertain, completely lost, and the man stepped out of the shadows behind her.

She felt him before she heard him, and gooseflesh covered her skin as she turned to look at him.

Still, she didn't know.

She couldn't have known.

She was unable to think, unable to figure out why the fuck she was suddenly sobbing.

He stood there, dressed in black, covered with silver blades.

Watching her.

He opened his arms.

"Don't cry," he said. "Don't cry, sweet thing."

Books in the Rune Alexander series—

Shiv Crew, book one
Blood and Bite, book two
Strange Trouble, book three
Obsidian Wings, book four
New Regime, book five
Wormwood Echoes, book six
The Witch's Daughter, book seven, in progress

From the author—

Authors need reviews like vampires need blood! If you've enjoyed this book, would you consider rating it and reviewing it on Amazon.com?

-Laken

ABOUT THE AUTHOR

Laken Cane is the author of the Rune Alexander books, a dark urban fantasy series. She lives in Ohio.

Visit her official website at www.lakencane.com and her friendly Facebook page at www.facebook.com/laken.cane.3

Printed in Great Britain
by Amazon